TROUT FISHING IN AMERICA

Richard Brautigan was born in the Pacific North-West in 1935. His novels include <u>Trout Fishing in America</u>, <u>In Watermelon Sugar</u> and <u>A Confederate General from Big Sur</u>. He has also written <u>Revenge of the Lawn</u>, a collection of short stories, and <u>The Pill Versus the Springhill Mine Disaster</u>, a book of poems.

BY RICHARD BRAUTIGAN

Richard Brautigan

TROUT FISHING
IN AMERICA

VINTAGE

Published by Vintage 1997

2 4 6 8 10 9 7 5 3 1

Marston Bates, <u>Man in Nature</u>, 2nd ed.
© Prentice-Hall, Inc. 1964

This book was first published
in the United States of America by
Four Seasons Foundations in its Writing series
edited by Donald Allen

First published in Great Britain
by Jonathan Cape Ltd, 1970

Vintage
Random House, 20 Vauxhall Bridge Road,
London SW1V 2SA

Random House Australia (Pty) Limited
20 Alfred Street, Milsons Point, Sydney
New South Wales 2061, Australia

Random House New Zealand Limited
18 Poland Road, Glenfield,
Auckland 10, New Zealand

Random House South Africa (Pty) Limited
Endulini, 5A Jubilee Road, Parktown 2193,
South Africa

Random House UK Limited Reg. No. 954009

A CIP catalogue record for this book
is available from the British Library

ISBN 0 09 974771 5

Papers used by Random House UK Ltd are natural,
recyclable products made from wood grown in
sustainable forests. The manufacturing
processes conform to the environmental
regulations of the country of origin

Printed and bound in Great Britain by
Cox & Wyman, Reading, Berkshire

For Jack Spicer and Ron Loewinsohn

CONTENTS

There are seductions that should be
in the Smithsonian Institution,
right next to The Spirit of St Louis.

THE COVER FOR TROUT FISHING IN AMERICA

The cover for Trout Fishing in America is a
photograph taken late in the afternoon, a
photograph of the Benjamin Franklin statue in
San Francisco's Washington Square.
  Born 1706-Died 1790, Benjamin Franklin stands
on a pedestal that looks like a house containing
stone furniture. He holds some papers in one
hand and his hat in the other.
  Then the statue speaks, saying in marble:

                    PRESENTED BY
                    H.D. COGSWELL
                       TO OUR
                    BOYS AND GIRLS
                    WHO WILL SOON
                    TAKE OUR PLACES
                    AND PASS ON.

Around the base of the statue are four words
facing the directions of this world, to the east
WELCOME, to the west WELCOME, to the north
WELCOME, to the south WELCOME. Just behind the

statue are three poplar trees, almost leafless
except for the top branches. The statue stands
in front of the middle tree. All around the
grass is wet from the rains of early February.
/ In the background is a tall cypress tree,
almost dark like a room. Adlai Stevenson
spoke under the tree in 1956, before a crowd
of 40,000 people.

There is a tall church across the street from
the statue with crosses, steeples, bells and a
vast door that looks like a huge mousehole,
perhaps from a Tom and Jerry cartoon, and
written above the door is 'Per L'Universo'.

Around five o'clock in the afternoon of my
cover for Trout Fishing in America, people
gather in the park across the street from the
church and they are hungry.

It's sandwich time for the poor.

But they cannot cross the street until the
signal is given. Then they all run across the
street to the church and get their sandwiches
that are wrapped in newspaper. They go
back to the park and unwrap the newspaper and
see what their sandwiches are all about.

A friend of mine unwrapped his sandwich one
afternoon and looked inside to find just a
leaf of spinach. That was all.

Was it Kafka who learned about America
by reading the autobiography of Benjamin
Franklin ...

Kafka who said, 'I like the Americans because
they are healthy and optimistic.'

KNOCK ON WOOD (PART ONE)

As a child when did I first hear about trout
fishing in America? From whom? I guess it
was a stepfather of mine.

Summer of 1942.

The old drunk told me about trout fishing.
When he could talk, he had a way of describing
trout as if they were a precious and
intelligent metal.

Silver is not a good adjective to describe
what I felt when he told me about trout fishing.

I'd like to get it right.

Maybe trout steel. Steel made from trout.
The clear snow-filled river acting as foundry
and heat.

Imagine Pittsburgh.

A steel that comes from trout, used to make
buildings, trains and tunnels.

The Andrew Carnegie of Trout!

The Reply of Trout Fishing in America:

I remember with particular amusement, people
with three-cornered hats fishing in the dawn.

KNOCK ON WOOD (PART TWO)

One spring afternoon as a child in the
strange town of Portland, I walked down to a
different street corner, and saw a row of
old houses, huddled together like seals on a
rock. Then there was a long field that came
sloping down off a hill. The field was
covered with green grass and bushes. On top of
the hill there was a grove of tall, dark trees.
At a distance I saw a waterfall come
pouring down off the hill. It was long and
white and I could almost feel its cold spray.

There must be a creek there, I thought, and it
probably has trout in it.

Trout.

At last an opportunity to go trout fishing,
to catch my first trout, to behold Pittsburgh.

It was growing dark. I didn't have time to go
and look at the creek. I walked home past the
glass whiskers of the houses, reflecting
the downward rushing waterfalls of night.

The next day I would go trout fishing for
the first time. I would get up early and

4

eat my breakfast and go. I had heard that it
was better to go trout fishing early in
the morning. The trout were better for it. They
had something extra in the morning. I went
home to prepare for trout fishing in America.
I didn't have any fishing tackle, so I had
to fall back on corny fishing tackle.

Like a joke.

Why did the chicken cross the road?

I bent a pin and tied it on to a piece of
white string.

And slept.

The next morning I got up early and ate my
breakfast. I took a slice of white bread to use
for bait. I planned on making doughballs
from the soft centre of the bread and
putting them on my vaudevillean hook.

I left the place and walked down to the
different street corner. How beautiful the field
looked and the creek that came pouring down
in a waterfall off the hill.

But as I got closer to the creek I could
see that something was wrong. The creek did not
act right. There was a strangeness to it.
There was a thing about its motion that was
wrong. Finally I got close enough to see what
the trouble was.

The waterfall was just a flight of white
wooden stairs leading up to a house in
the trees.

I stood there for a long time, looking up and
looking down, following the stairs with my
eyes, having trouble believing.

Then I knocked on my creek and heard the
sound of wood.

I ended up by being my own trout and eating
the slice of bread myself.

The Reply of Trout Fishing in America:

There was nothing I could do. I couldn't
change a flight of stairs into a creek.
The boy walked back to where he came from. The
same thing once happened to me. I remember
mistaking an old woman for a trout stream in
Vermont, and I had to beg her pardon.

'Excuse me,' I said. 'I thought you were a
trout stream.'

'I'm not,' she said.

RED LIP

Seventeen years later I sat on a rock. It was
under a tree next to an old abandoned shack that
had a sheriff's notice nailed like a funeral
wreath to the front door.

NO TRESPASSING
4/17 OF A HAIKU

Many rivers had flowed past those seventeen
years, and thousands of trout, and now
beside the highway and the sheriff's notice
flowed yet another river, the Klamath, and I was
trying to get thirty-five miles downstream to
Steelhead, the place where I was staying.
It was all very simple. No one would stop
and pick me up even though I was carrying
fishing tackle. People usually stop and
pick up a fisherman. I had to wait three hours
for a ride.
The sun was like a huge fifty-cent piece that
someone had poured kerosene on and then had
lit with a match and said, 'Here, hold

this while I go get a newspaper,' and put the
coin in my hand, but never came back.

I had walked for miles and miles until I came
to the rock under the tree and sat down.
Every time a car would come by, about once
every ten minutes, I would get up and
stick out my thumb as if it were a bunch of
bananas and then sit back down on the rock
again.

The old shack had a tin roof coloured reddish
by years of wear, like a hat worn under the
guillotine. A corner of the roof was loose and a
hot wind blew down the river and the loose
corner clanged in the wind.

A car went by. An old couple. The car
almost swerved off the road and into the river.
I guess they didn't see many hitchhikers up
there. The car went around the corner with
both of them looking back at me.

I had nothing else to do, so I caught
salmon flies in my landing net. I made up my own
game. It went like this: I couldn't chase after
them. I had to let them fly to me. It was
something to do with my mind. I caught six.

A little ways up from the shack was an outhouse with its door flung violently open.
The inside of the outhouse was exposed
like a human face and the outhouse seemed to
say, 'The old guy who built me crapped in
here 9,745 times and he's dead now and I
don't want anyone else to touch me. He was a
good guy. He built me with loving care. Leave
me alone. I'm a monument now to a good ass
gone under. There's no mystery here. That's
why the door's open. If you have to crap,
go in the bushes like the deer.'

'Fuck you,' I said to the outhouse. 'All I
want is a ride down the river.'

8

THE KOOL-AID WINO

When I was a child I had a friend who became a
Kool-Aid wino as the result of a rupture.
He was a member of a very large and poor
German family. All the older children in the
family had to work in the fields during the
summer, picking beans for two-and-one-half cents
a pound to keep the family going. Everyone
worked except my friend who couldn't because
he was ruptured. There was no money for
an operation. There wasn't even enough money to
buy him a truss. So he stayed home and became
a Kool-Aid wino.
  One morning in August I went over to his
house. He was still in bed. He looked up at
me from underneath a tattered revolution
of old blankets. He had never slept under
a sheet in his life.
  'Did you bring the nickel you promised?' he
asked.
  'Yeah,' I said. 'It's here in my pocket.'
  'Good.'
  He hopped out of bed and he was already

9

dressed. He had told me once that he never took
off his clothes when he went to bed.

'Why bother?' he had said. 'You're only going
to get up, anyway. Be prepared for it.
You're not fooling anyone by taking your clothes
off when you go to bed.'

He went into the kitchen, stepping around the
littlest children, whose wet diapers were
in various stages of anarchy. He made his
breakfast: a slice of homemade bread covered
with Karo syrup and peanut butter.

'Let's go,' he said.

We left the house with him still eating the
sandwich. The store was three blocks away,
on the other side of a field covered with heavy
yellow grass. There were many pheasants in the
field. Fat with summer they barely flew away
when we came up to them.

'Hello,' said the grocer. He was bald with a
red birthmark on his head. The birthmark
looked just like an old car parked on his head.
He automatically reached for a package of
grape Kool-Aid and put it on the counter.

'Five cents.'

'He's got it,' my friend said.

I reached into my pocket and gave the nickel
to the grocer. He nodded and the old red car
wobbled back and forth on the road as if the
driver were having an epileptic seizure.

We left.

My friend led the way across the field. One of
the pheasants didn't even bother to fly. He
ran across the field in front of us like
a feathered pig.

When we got back to my friend's house the
ceremony began. To him the making of Kool-Aid
was a romance and a ceremony. It had to
be performed in an exact manner and with dignity.

10

First he got a gallon jar and we went around
to the side of the house where the water
spigot thrust itself out of the ground like the
finger of a saint, surrounded by a mud puddle.

He opened the Kool-Aid and dumped it into the
jar. Putting the jar under the spigot, he turned
the water on. The water spit, splashed and
guzzled out of the spigot.

He was careful to see that the jar did not
overflow and the precious Kool-Aid spill
out on to the ground. When the jar was full he
turned the water off with a sudden but
delicate motion like a famous brain surgeon
removing a disordered portion of the
imagination. Then he screwed the lid tightly
on to the top of the jar and gave it a good
shake.

The first part of the ceremony was over.

Like the inspired priest of an exotic cult, he
had performed the first part of the
ceremony well.

His mother came around the side of the
house and said in a voice filled with sand and
string, 'When are you going to do the
dishes? . . . Huh?'

'Soon,' he said.

'Well, you better,' she said.

When she left, it was as if she had never
been there at all. The second part of the
ceremony began with him carrying the jar very
carefully to an abandoned chicken house in
the back. 'The dishes can wait,' he said to me.
Bertrand Russell could not have stated it
better.

He opened the chicken house door and we went
in. The place was littered with half-rotten
comic books. They were like fruit under a tree.
In the corner was an old mattress and

11

beside the mattress were four quart jars. He took
the gallon jar over to them, and filled them
carefully not spilling a drop. He screwed their
caps on tightly and was now ready for a
day's drinking.

You're supposed to make only two quarts of
Kool-Aid from a package, but he always made a
gallon, so his Kool-Aid was a mere shadow
of its desired potency. And you're supposed to
add a cup of sugar to every package of Kool-Aid,
but he never put any sugar in his Kool-Aid
because there wasn't any sugar to put in it.

He created his own Kool-Aid reality and was
able to illuminate himself by it.

ANOTHER METHOD OF MAKING WALNUT CATSUP

And this is a very small cookbook for Trout
Fishing in America as if Trout Fishing in
America were a rich gourmet and Trout Fishing in
America had Maria Callas for a girlfriend
and they ate together on a marble table with
beautiful candles.

Compote of Apples

Take a dozen of golden pippins, pare them
nicely and take the core out with a small
penknife; put them into some water, and
let them be well scalded; then take a little
of the water with some sugar, and a few
apples which may be sliced into it, and
let the whole boil till it comes to a syrup;
then pour it over your pippins, and garnish
them with dried cherries and lemon-peel
cut fine. You must take care that your
pippins are not split.

And Maria Callas sang to Trout Fishing in

America as they ate their apples together.

A Standing Crust for Great Pies

Take a peck of flour and six pounds of
butter boiled in a gallon of water: skim it
off into the flour, and as little of the
liquor as you can. Work it up well into a
paste, and then pull it into pieces till it
is cold. Then make it up into what form you
please.

And Trout Fishing in America smiled at
Maria Callas as they ate their pie crust
together.

A Spoonful Pudding

Take a spoonful of flour, a spoonful of
cream or milk, an egg, a little nutmeg,
ginger, and salt. Mix all together, and
boil it in a little wooden dish half an
hour. If you think proper you may add a few
currants.

And Trout Fishing in America said, 'The moon's
coming out.' And Maria Callas said, 'Yes,
it is.'

Another Method of Making Walnut Catsup

Take green walnuts before the shell is
formed, and grind them in a crab-mill,
or pound them in a marble mortar.
Squeeze out the juice through a coarse
cloth, and put to every gallon of juice
a pound of anchovies, and the same
quantity of bay-salt, four ounces of

Jamaica pepper, two of long and two of
black pepper; of mace, cloves, and
ginger, each an ounce, and a stick of
horseradish. Boil all together till
reduced to half the quantity, and then
put it into a pot. When it is cold, bottle
it close, and in three months it will be
fit for use.

And Trout Fishing in America and Maria Callas
poured walnut catsup on their hamburgers.

PROLOGUE TO GRIDER CREEK

Mooresville, Indiana, is the town that John
Dillinger came from, and the town has a
John Dillinger Museum. You can go in and look
around.

Some towns are known as the peach capital of
America or the cherry capital or the oyster
capital, and there's always a festival and the
photograph of a pretty girl in a bathing suit.

Mooresville, Indiana, is the John Dillinger
capital of America.

Recently a man moved there with his wife, and
he discovered hundreds of rats in his
basement. They were huge, slow-moving child-eyed
rats.

When his wife had to visit some of her
relatives for a few days, the man went out and
bought a .38 revolver and a lot of ammunition.
Then he went down to the basement where the
rats were, and he started shooting them. It
didn't bother the rats at all. They acted
as if it were a movie and started eating their
dead companions for popcorn.

The man walked over to a rat that was busy
eating a friend and placed the pistol against
the rat's head. The rat did not move and
continued eating away. When the hammer clicked
back, the rat paused between bites and looked
out of the corner of its eye. First at the
pistol and then at the man. It was a kind of
friendly look as if to say, 'When my mother was
young she sang like Deanna Durbin.'

The man pulled the trigger.

He had no sense of humour.

There's always a single feature, a double
feature and an eternal feature playing at the
Great Theater in Mooresville, Indiana: the
John Dillinger capital of America.

GRIDER CREEK

I had heard there was some good fishing in
there and it was running clear while all the
other large creeks were running muddy from the
snow melting off the Marble Mountains.

I also heard there were some Eastern brook
trout in there, high up in the mountains, living
in the wakes of beaver dams.

The guy who drove the school bus drew a map of
Grider Creek, showing where the good fishing
was. We were standing in front of Steelhead
Lodge when he drew the map. It was a very
hot day. I'd imagine it was a hundred degrees.

You had to have a car to get to Grider Creek
where the good fishing was, and I didn't have
a car. The map was nice, though. Drawn with
a heavy dull pencil on a piece of paper bag.
With a little square ☐ for a sawmill.

THE BALLET FOR TROUT FISHING IN AMERICA

How the Cobra Lily traps insects is a ballet for
Trout Fishing in America, a ballet to be
performed at the University of California at
Los Angeles.

The plant is beside me here on the back porch.

It died a few days after I bought it at
Woolworth's. That was months ago, during the
presidential election of nineteen hundred
and sixty.

I buried the plant in an empty Metrecal can.

The side of the can says, 'Metrecal Dietary
for Weight Control,' and below that reads,
'Ingredients: Non-fat milk solids, soya flour,
whole milk solids, sucrose, starch, corn oil,
coconut oil, yeast, imitation vanilla,'
but the can's only a graveyard now for a
Cobra Lily that has turned dry and brown and has
black freckles.

As a kind of funeral wreath, there is a red,
white and blue button sticking in the plant
and the words on it say, 'I'm for Nixon'.

The main energy for the ballet comes from a

19

description of the Cobra Lily. The description
could be used as a welcome mat on the front
porch of hell or to conduct an orchestra of
mortuaries with ice-cold woodwinds or be an
atomic mailman in the pines, in the pines
where the sun never shines.

'Nature has endowed the Cobra Lily with the
means of catching its own food. The forked
tongue is covered with honey glands which
attract the insects upon which it feeds. Once
inside the hood, downward pointing hairs prevent
the insect from crawling out. The digestive
liquids are found in the base of the plant.

'The supposition that it is necessary to feed
the Cobra Lily a piece of hamburger or an
insect daily is erroneous.'

I hope the dancers do a good job of it, they
hold our imagination in their feet, dancing
in Los Angeles for Trout Fishing in America.

A WALDEN POND FOR WINOS

The autumn carried along with it, like the
roller coaster of a flesh-eating plant,
port wine and the people who drank that dark
sweet wine, people long since gone, except
for me.

Always wary of the police, we drank in the
safest place we could find, the park across
from the church.

There were three poplar trees in the middle of
the park and there was a statue of Benjamin
Franklin in front of the trees. We sat there
and drank port.

At home my wife was pregnant.

I would call on the telephone after I
finished work and say, 'I won't be home for a
little while. I'm going to have a drink with
some friends.'

The three of us huddled in the park, talking.
They were both broken-down artists from New
Orleans where they had drawn pictures of
tourists in Pirate's Alley.

Now in San Francisco, with the cold autumn

wind upon them, they had decided that the
future held only two directions: They were
either going to open up a flea circus or
commit themselves to an insane asylum.

So they talked about it while they drank wine.

They talked about how to make little clothes
for fleas by pasting pieces of coloured paper
on their backs.

They said the way that you trained fleas
was to make them dependent upon you for their
food. This was done by letting them feed off
you at an appointed hour.

They talked about making little flea wheel-
barrows and pool tables and bicycles.

They would charge fifty-cents admission for
their flea circus. The business was certain to
have a future to it. Perhaps they would even
get on the Ed Sullivan Show.

They of course did not have their fleas yet,
but they could easily be obtained from a
white cat.

Then they decided that the fleas that lived on
Siamese cats would probably be more intelligent
than the fleas that lived on just ordinary alley
cats. It only made sense that drinking
intelligent blood would make intelligent fleas.

And so it went on until it was exhausted and
we went and bought another fifth of port
wine and returned to the trees and Benjamin
Franklin.

Now it was close to sunset and the earth was
beginning to cool off in the correct manner
of eternity and office girls were returning like
penguins from Montgomery Street. They looked
at us hurriedly and mentally registered: winos.

Then the two artists talked about
committing themselves to an insane asylum for
the winter. They talked about how warm it would

22

be in the insane asylum, with television,
clean sheets on soft beds, hamburger gravy
over mashed potatoes, a dance once a week
with the lady kooks, clean clothes, a locked
razor and lovely young student nurses.

Ah, yes, there was a future in the insane
asylum. No winter spent there could be a
total loss.

TOM MARTIN CREEK

I walked down one morning from Steelhead,
following the Klamath River that was high and
murky and had the intelligence of a dinosaur.
Tom Martin Creek was a small creek with
cold, clear water and poured out of a canyon
and through a culvert under the highway and then
into the Klamath.

I dropped a fly in a small pool just below
where the creek flowed out of the culvert and
took a nine-inch trout. It was a good-looking
fish and fought all over the top of the pool.

Even though the creek was very small and
poured out of a steep brushy canyon filled
with poison oak, I decided to follow the creek
up a ways because I liked the feel and
motion of the creek.

I liked the name, too.

Tom Martin Creek.

It's good to name creeks after people and then
later to follow them for a while seeing what
they have to offer, what they know and have
made of themselves.

But that creek turned out to be a real
son-of-a-bitch. I had to fight it all the
God-damn way: brush, poison oak and hardly any
good places to fish, and sometimes the
canyon was so narrow the creek poured out like
water from a faucet. Sometimes it was so bad
that it just left me standing there, not
knowing which way to jump.

You had to be a plumber to fish that creek.

After that first trout I was alone in there.
But I didn't know it until later.

TROUT FISHING ON THE BEVEL

The two graveyards were next to each other on
small hills and between them flowed Graveyard
Creek, a slow-moving, funeral-procession-on-a-
hot-day creek with a lot of fine trout in it.

And the dead didn't mind me fishing there at
all.

One graveyard had tall fir trees growing in
it, and the grass was kept Peter Pan green
all year round by pumping water up from
the creek, and the graveyard had fine marble
headstones and statues and tombs.

The other graveyard was for the poor and it
had no trees and the grass turned a flat-tyre
brown in the summer and stayed that way until
the rain, like a mechanic, began in the
late autumn.

There were no fancy headstones for the poor
dead. Their markers were small boards that
looked like heels of stale bread:

Devoted Slob Father Of

Beloved Worked-to-Death Mother Of

On some of the graves were fruit jars and tin
cans with wilted flowers in them:

Sacred

To the Memory

of

John Talbot

Who at the Age of Eighteen

Had His Ass Shot Out

In a Honky-Tonk

November 1, 1936

This Mayonnaise Jar

With Wilted Flowers In It

Was Left Here Six Months Ago

By His Sister

Who Is In

The Crazy Place Now.

Eventually the seasons would take care of
their wooden names like a sleepy short-order
cook cracking eggs over a grill next to a
railroad station. Whereas the well-to-do would

have their names for a long time written on
marble hors d'oeuvres like horses trotting up
the fancy paths to the sky.

I fished Graveyard Creek in the dusk when the
hatch was on and worked some good trout out
of there. Only the poverty of the dead
bothered me.

Once, while cleaning the trout before I went
home in the almost night, I had a vision of
going over to the poor graveyard and
gathering up grass and fruit jars and tin cans
and markers and wilted flowers and bugs and
weeds and clods and going home and putting a
hook in the vice and tying a fly with all that
stuff and then going outside and casting it up
into the sky, watching it float over clouds and
then into the evening star.

SEA, SEA RIDER

The man who owned the bookstore was not magic.
He was not a three-legged crow on the
dandelion side of the mountain.

He was, of course, a Jew, a retired merchant
seaman who had been torpedoed in the North
Atlantic and floated there day after day until
death did not want him. He had a young wife,
a heart attack, a Volkswagen and a home in
Marin County. He liked the works of George
Orwell, Richard Aldington and Edmund Wilson.

He learned about life at sixteen, first from
Dostoevsky and then from the whores of New
Orleans.

The bookstore was a parking lot for used
graveyards. Thousands of graveyards were parked
in rows like cars. Most of the books were out
of print, and no one wanted to read them
any more and the people who had read the books
had died or forgotten about them, but through
the organic process of music the books had
become virgins again. They wore their ancient
copyrights like new maidenheads.

I went to the bookstore in the afternoons
after I got off work, during that terrible year
of 1959.

He had a kitchen in the back of the store and
he brewed cups of thick Turkish coffee in a
copper pan. I drank coffee and read old
books and waited for the year to end. He had a
small room above the kitchen.

It looked down on the bookstore and had
Chinese screens in front of it. The room
contained a couch, a glass cabinet with Chinese
things in it and a table and three chairs.
There was a tiny bathroom fastened like a
watch fob to the room.

I was sitting on a stool in the bookstore one
afternoon reading a book that was in the shape
of a chalice. The book had clear pages like
gin, and the first page in the book read:

Billy

the Kid

born

November 23,

1859

in

New York

City

The owner of the bookstore came up to me, and
put his arm on my shoulder and said, 'Would
you like to get laid?' His voice was very kind.

'No,' I said.

'You're wrong,' he said, and then without
saying anything else, he went out in front

of the bookstore, and stopped a pair of total
strangers, a man and a woman. He talked to
them for a few moments. I couldn't hear what he
was saying. He pointed at me in the bookstore.
The woman nodded her head and then the man
nodded his head.

They came into the bookstore.

I was embarrassed. I could not leave the
bookstore because they were entering by the only
door, so I decided to go upstairs and go to
the toilet. I got up abruptly and walked
to the back of the bookstore and went upstairs
to the bathroom, and they followed after me.

I could hear them on the stairs.

I waited for a long time in the bathroom and
they waited an equally long time in the
other room. They never spoke. When I came out
of the bathroom, the woman was lying naked
on the couch, and man was sitting in a chair
with his hat on his lap.

'Don't worry about him,' the girl said. 'These
things make no difference to him. He's rich.
He has 3,859 Rolls-Royces.' The girl was very
pretty and her body was like a clear
mountain river of skin and muscle flowing over
rocks of bone and hidden nerves.

'Come to me,' she said. 'And come inside me
for we are Aquarius and I love you.'

I looked at the man sitting in the chair.
He was not smiling and he did not look sad.

I took off my shoes and all my clothes. The
man did not say a word.

The girl's body moved ever so slightly from
side to side.

There was nothing else I could do for my body
was like birds sitting on a telephone wire
strung out down the world, clouds tossing the
wires carefully.

31

I laid the girl.

It was like the eternal 59th second when it becomes a minute and then looks kind of sheepish.

'Good,' the girl said, and kissed me on the face.

The man sat there without speaking or moving or sending out any emotion into the room. I guess he <u>was</u> rich and owned 3,859 Rolls-Royces.

Afterwards the girl got dressed and she and the man left. They walked down the stairs and on their way out, I heard him say his first words.

'Would you like to go to Ernie's for dinner?'

'I don't know,' the girl said. 'It's a little early to think about dinner.'

Then I heard the door close and they were gone. I got dressed and went downstairs. The flesh about my body felt soft and relaxed like an experiment in functional background music.

The owner of the bookstore was sitting at his desk behind the counter. 'I'll tell you what happened up there,' he said, in a beautiful anti-three-legged-crow voice, in an anti-dandelion side of the mountain voice.

'What?' I said.

'You fought in the Spanish Civil War. You were a young Communist from Cleveland, Ohio. She was a painter. A New York Jew who was sightseeing in the Spanish Civil War as if it were the Mardi Gras in New Orleans being acted out by Greek statues.

'She was drawing a picture of a dead anarchist when you met her. She asked you to stand beside the anarchist and act as if you had killed him. You slapped her across the face and said something that would be embarrassing for me to repeat.

'You both fell very much in love.

32

'Once while you were at the front she read
Anatomy of Melancholy and did 349 drawings
of a lemon.

'Your love for each other was mostly
spiritual. Neither one of you performed like
millionaires in bed.

'When Barcelona fell, you and she flew to
England, and then took a ship back to New
York. Your love for each other remained in
Spain. It was only a war love. You loved only
yourselves, loving each other in Spain during
the war. On the Atlantic you were different
towards each other and became every day more and
more like people lost from each other.

'Every wave on the Atlantic was like a dead
seagull dragging its driftwood artillery from
horizon to horizon.

'When the ship bumped up against America, you
departed without saying anything and never
saw each other again. The last I heard of you,
you were still living in Philadelphia.'

'That's what you think happened up there?' I
said.

'Partly,' he said. 'Yes, that's part of it.'

He took out his pipe and filled it with
tobacco and lit it.

'Do you want me to tell you what else
happened up there?' he said.

'Go ahead.'

'You crossed the border into Mexico,' he said.
'You rode your horse into a small town. The
people knew who you were and they were afraid of
you. They knew you had killed many men with
that gun you wore at your side. The town itself
was so small that it didn't have a priest.

'When the rurales saw you, they left the town.
Tough as they were, they did not want to have
anything to do with you. The rurales left.

'You became the most powerful man in town.

'You were seduced by a thirteen-year-old girl,
and you and she lived together in an adobe
hut, and practically all you did was make love.

'She was slender and had long dark hair. You
made love standing, sitting, lying on the
dirt floor with pigs and chickens around you.
The walls, the floor and even the roof of the
hut were coated with your sperm and her come.

'You slept on the floor at night and used your
sperm for a pillow and her come for a blanket.

'The people in the town were so afraid of
you that they could do nothing.

'After a while she started going around town
without any clothes on, and the people of the
town said that it was not a good thing, and
when you started going around without any
clothes, and when both of you began making love
on the back of your horse in the middle of the
zocalo, the people of the town became so
afraid that they abandoned the town. It's been
abandoned ever since.

'People won't live there.

'Neither of you lived to be twenty-one. It was
not necessary.

'See, I do know what happened upstairs,' he
said. He smiled at me kindly. His eyes were like
the shoelaces of a harpsichord.

I thought about what happened upstairs.

'You know what I say is the truth,' he said.
'For you saw it with your own eyes and travelled
it with your own body. Finish the book you
were reading before you were interrupted.
I'm glad you got laid.'

Once resumed, the pages of the book began to
speed up and turn faster and faster until
they were spinning like wheels in the sea.

34

THE LAST YEAR THE TROUT CAME UP HAYMAN CREEK

Gone now the old fart. Hayman Creek was named
for Charles Hayman, a sort of half-assed
pioneer in a country that not many wanted to
live in because it was poor and ugly and
horrible. He built a shack, this was in 1876, on
a little creek that drained a worthless hill.
After a while the creek was called Hayman Creek.

Mr Hayman did not know how to read or write
and considered himself better for it.
Mr Hayman did odd jobs for years and years and
years and years.

Your mule's broke?
Get Mr Hayman to fix it.
Your fences are on fire?
Get Mr Hayman to put them out.

Mr Hayman lived on a diet of stone-ground
wheat and kale. He bought the wheat by the
hundred-pound sack and ground it himself with a
mortar and pestle. He grew the kale in front
of his shack and tended the kale as if it were
prize-winning orchids.

During all the time that was his life, Mr

Hayman never had a cup of coffee, a smoke, a drink
or a woman and thought he'd be a fool if he did.

In the winter a few trout would go up Hayman
Creek, but by early summer the creek was almost
dry and there were no fish in it.

Mr Hayman used to catch a trout or two and eat
raw trout with his stone-ground wheat and his
kale, and then one day he was so old that he did
not feel like working any more, and he
looked so old that the children thought he must
be evil to live by himself, and they were afraid
to go up the creek near his shack.

It didn't bother Mr Hayman. The last thing in
the world he had any use for were children.
Reading and writing and children were all the
same, Mr Hayman thought, and ground his wheat
and tended his kale and caught a trout or two
when they were in the creek.

He looked ninety years old for thirty years
and then he got the notion that he would die,
and did so. The year he died the trout didn't
come up Hayman Creek, and never went up the
creek again. With the old man dead, the trout
figured it was better to stay where they were.

The mortar and pestle fell off the shelf and
broke.

The shack rotted away.

And the weeds grew into the kale.

Twenty years after Mr Hayman's death, some
fish and game people were planting trout in the
streams around there.

'Might as well put some here,' one of the men
said.

'Sure,' the other one said.

They dumped a can full of trout in the
creek and no sooner had the trout touched the
water, than they turned their white bellies up
and floated dead down the creek.

TROUT DEATH BY PORT WINE

It was not an outhouse resting upon the
imagination.

It was reality.

An eleven-inch rainbow trout was killed. Its
life taken forever from the waters of the
earth, by giving it a drink of port wine.

It is against the natural order of death for a
trout to die by having a drink of port wine.

It is all right for a trout to have its neck
broken by a fisherman and then to be tossed
into the creel or for a trout to die from a
fungus that crawls like sugar-coloured ants
over its body until the trout is in death's
sugarbowl.

It is all right for a trout to be trapped in
a pool that dries up in the late summer or to
be caught in the talons of a bird or the claws
of an animal.

Yes, it is even all right for a trout to be
killed by pollution, to die in a river of
suffocating human excrement.

There are trout that die of old age and their

white beards flow to the sea.

All these things are in the natural order of death, but for a trout to die from a drink of port wine, that is another thing.

No mention of it in 'The treatyse of fysshynge wyth an angle,' in the Boke of St Albans, published 1496. No mention of it in Minor Tactics of the Chalk Stream, by H.C. Cutcliffe, published in 1910. No mention of it in Truth Is Stranger than Fishin', by Beatrice Cook, published in 1955. No mention of it in Northern Memoirs, by Richard Franck, published in 1694. No mention of it in I Go A-Fishing, by W.C. Prime, published in 1873. No mention of it in Trout Fishing and Trout Flies, by Jim Quick, published in 1957. No mention of it in Certaine Experiments Concerning Fish and Fruite, by John Taverner, published in 1600. No mention of it in A River Never Sleeps, by Roderick L. Haig Brown, published in 1946. No mention of it in Till Fish Us Do Part, by Beatrice Cook, published in 1949. No mention of it in The Flyfisher & the Trout's Point of View, by Col. E.W. Harding, published in 1931. No mention of it in Chalk Stream Studies, by Charles Kingsley, published in 1859. No mention of it in Trout Madness, by Robert Traver, published in 1960.

No mention of it in Sunshine and the Dry Fly, by J.W. Dunne, published in 1924. No mention of it in Just Fishing, by Ray Berman, published in 1932. No mention of it in Matching the Hatch, by Ernest G. Schwiebert, Jr, published in 1955. No mention of it in The Art of Trout

Fishing on Rapid Streams, by H.C. Cutcliffe, published in 1863. No mention of it in Old Flies in New Dresses, by C.E. Walker, published in 1898. No mention of it in Fisherman's Spring, by Roderick L. Haig-Brown, published in 1951. No mention of it in The Determined Angler and the Brook Trout, by Charles Bradford, published in 1916. No mention of it in Woman Can Fish, by Chisie Farrington, published in 1951. No mention of it in Tales of the Angler's El Dorado New Zealand, by Zane Grey, published in 1926. No mention of it in The Flyfisher's Guide, by G.C. Bainbridge, published in 1816.

There's no mention of a trout dying by having a drink of port wine anywhere.

To describe the Supreme Executioner: We woke up in the morning and it was dark outside. He came kind of smiling into the kitchen and we ate breakfast.

Fried potatoes and eggs and coffee.

'Well, you old bastard,' he said. 'Pass the salt.'

The tackle was already in the car, so we just got in and drove away. Beginning at the first light of dawn, we hit the road at the bottom of the mountains, and drove up into the dawn.

The light behind the trees was like going into a gradual and strange department store.

'That was a good-looking girl last night,' he said.

'Yeah,' I said. 'You did all right.'

'If the shoe fits . . .' he said.

Owl Snuff Creek was just a small creek, only a few miles long, but there were some nice

trout in it. We got out of the car and walked
a quarter of a mile down the mountainside
to the creek. I put my tackle together. He
pulled a pint of port wine out of his jacket
pocket and said, 'Wouldn't you know.'

'No thanks,' I said.

He took a good snort and then shook his head,
side to side, and said, 'Do you know what this
creek reminds me of?'

'No,' I said, tying a grey and yellow fly on
to my leader.

'It reminds me of Evangeline's vagina, a
constant dream of my childhood and promoter
of my youth.'

'That's nice,' I said.

'Longfellow was the Henry Miller of my
childhood,' he said.

'Good,' I said.

I cast into a little pool that had a swirl of
fir needles going around the edge of it. The
fir needles went around and around. It made
no sense that they should come from trees. They
looked perfectly contented and natural in the
pool as if the pool had grown them on watery
branches.

I had a good hit on my third cast, but
missed it.

'Oh, boy,' he said. 'I think I'll watch you
fish. The stolen painting is in the house
next door.'

I fished upstream coming ever closer and
closer to the narrow staircase of the
canyon. Then I went up into it as if I were
entering a department store. I caught three
trout in the lost and found department.
He didn't even put his tackle together. He just
followed after me, drinking port wine and poking
a stick at the world.

'This is a beautiful creek,' he said. 'It
reminds me of Evangeline's hearing aid.'
We ended up at a large pool that was formed by
the creek crashing through the children's
toy section. At the beginning of the pool the
water was like cream, then it mirrored out
and reflected the shadow of a large tree.
By this time the sun was up. You could see it
coming down the mountain.
I cast into the cream and let my fly drift
down on to a long branch of the tree, next to a
bird.
Go-wham!
I set the hook and the trout started jumping.
'Giraffe races at Kilimanjaro!' he shouted,
and every time the trout jumped, he jumped.
'Bee races at Mount Everest!' he shouted.
I didn't have a net with me so I fought the
trout over to the edge of the creek and swung
it up on to the shore.
The trout had a big red stripe down its side.
It was a good rainbow.
'What a beauty,' he said.
He picked it up and it was squirming in his
hands.
'Break its neck,' I said.
'I have a better idea,' he said. 'Before I
kill it, let me at least soothe its approach
into death. This trout needs a drink.' He
took the bottle of port out of his pocket,
unscrewed the cap and poured a good slug into
the trout's mouth.
The trout went into a spasm.
Its body shook very rapidly like a telescope
during an earthquake. The mouth was wide open
and chattering almost as if it had human teeth.
He laid the trout on a white rock, head down,
and some of the wine trickled out of its

41

mouth and made a stain on the rock.
  The trout was lying very still now.
  'It died happy,' he said.
  'This is my ode to Alcoholics Anonymous.
  'Look here!'

THE AUTOPSY OF TROUT FISHING IN AMERICA

This is the autopsy of Trout Fishing in America
as if Trout Fishing in America had been
Lord Byron and had died in Missolonghi, Greece,
and afterwards never saw the shores of
Idaho again, never saw Carrie Creek, Worsewick
Hot Springs, Paradise Creek, Salt Creek and
Duck Lake again.

The Autopsy of Trout Fishing in America:
'The body was in excellent state and
appeared as one that had died suddenly of
asphyxiation. The bony cranial vault was opened
and the bones of the cranium were found very
hard without any traces of the sutures like
the bones of a person 80 years, so much so
that one would have said that the cranium
was formed by one solitary bone ... The
meninges were attached to the internal walls of
the cranium so firmly that while sawing the
bone around the interior to detach the bone from
the dura the strength of two robust men was
not sufficient ... The cerebrum with
cerebellum weighed about six medical pounds.

The kidneys were very large but healthy
and the urinary bladder was relatively small.'
   On May 2, 1824, the body of Trout Fishing in
America left Missolonghi by ship destined
to arrive in England on the evening of June 29,
1824.
   Trout Fishing in America's body was preserved
in a cask holding one hundred-eighty gallons
of spirits: O, a long way from Idaho, a long way
from Stanley Basin, Little Redfish Lake, the
Big Lost River and from Lake Josephus and
the Big Wood River.

THE MESSAGE

Last night a blue thing, the smoke itself, from
our campfire drifted down the valley,
entering into the sound of the bell-mare until
the blue thing and the bell could not be
separated, no matter how hard you tried. There
was no crowbar big enough to do the job.
   Yesterday afternoon we drove down the road
from Wells Summit, then we ran into the sheep.
They also were being moved on the road.
   A shepherd walked in front of the car, a leafy
branch in his hand, sweeping the sheep aside.
He looked like a young, skinny Adolf Hitler, but
friendly.
   I guess there were a thousand sheep on the
road. It was hot and dusty and noisy and took
what seemed like a long time.
   At the end of the sheep was a covered wagon
being pulled by two horses. There was a third
horse, the bell-mare, tied on the back of the
wagon. The white canvas rippled in the wind
and the wagon had no driver. The seat was empty.
   Finally the Adolf Hitler, but friendly,

shepherd got the last of them out of the way.
He smiled and we waved and said thank you.

We were looking for a good place to camp.
We drove down the road, following the
Little Smoky about five miles and didn't see a
place that we liked, so we decided to turn
around and go back to a place we had seen
just a ways up Carrie Creek.

'I hope those God-damn sheep aren't on the
road,' I said.

We drove back to where we had seen them
on the road and, of course, they were gone, but
as we drove on up the road, we just kept
following sheep shit. It was ahead of us for the
next mile.

I kept looking down on the meadow by the
Little Smoky, hoping to see the sheep down
there, but there wasn't a sheep in sight, only
the shit in front of us on the road.

As if it were a game invented by the sphincter
muscle, we knew what the score was. Shaking
our heads side to side, waiting.

Then we went around a bend and the sheep
burst like a roman candle all over the road
and again a thousand sheep and the shepherd in
front of us, wondering what the fuck. The same
thing was in our minds.

There was some beer in the back seat. It
wasn't exactly cold, but it wasn't warm either.
I tell you I was really embarrassed. I took a
bottle of beer and got out of the car.

I walked up to the shepherd who looked like
Adolf Hitler, but friendly.

'I'm sorry,' I said.

'It's the sheep,' he said. (O sweet and
distant blossoms of Munich and Berlin!)
'Sometimes they are a trouble but it all works
out.'

46

'Would you like a bottle of beer?' I said.
'I'm sorry to put you through this again.'
    'Thank you,' he said, shrugging his shoulders.
He took the beer over and put it on the empty
seat of the wagon. That's how it looked.
After a long time, we were free of the sheep.
They were like a net dragged finally away from
the car.
    We drove up to the place on Carrie Creek and
pitched the tent and took our goods out of the
car and piled them in the tent.
    Then we drove up the creek a ways, above the
place where there were beaver dams and the trout
stared back at us like fallen leaves.
    We filled the back of the car with wood for
the fire and I caught a mess of those leaves for
dinner. They were small and dark and cold.
The autumn was good to us.
    When we got back to our camp, I saw the
shepherd's wagon down the road a ways and on the
meadow I heard the bell-mare and the very
distant sound of the sheep.
    It was the final circle with the Adolf Hitler,
but friendly, shepherd as the diameter. He was
camping down there for the night. So in the
dusk, the blue smoke from our campfire
went down and got in there with the bell-mare.
    The sheep lulled themselves into senseless
sleep, one following another like the
banners of a lost army. I have here a very
important message that just arrived a few
moments ago. It says 'Stalingrad.'

TROUT FISHING IN AMERICA TERRORISTS

Long live our friend the revolver!
Long live our friend the machine gun!

- Israeli terrorist chant

One April morning in the sixth grade, we became,
first by accident and then by premeditation,
trout fishing in America terrorists.

It came about this way: we were a strange
bunch of kids.

We were always being called in before the
principal for daring and mischievous deeds. The
principal was a young man and a genius in the
way he handled us.

One April morning we were standing around in
the play yard, acting as if it were a huge
open-air poolhall with the first-graders coming
and going like pool balls. We were all bored
with the prospect of another day's school,
studying Cuba.

One of us had a piece of white chalk and as a
first-grader went walking by, the one of us

absent-mindedly wrote 'Trout fishing in
America' on the back of the first-grader.

The first-grader strained around, trying to
read what was written on his back, but he
couldn't see what it was, so he shrugged his
shoulders and went off to play on the swings.

We watched the first-grader walk away with
'Trout fishing in America' written on his back.
It looked good and seemed quite natural and
pleasing to the eye that a first-grader should
have 'Trout fishing in America' written in
chalk on his back.

The next time I saw a first-grader, I
borrowed my friend's piece of chalk and said,
'First-grader, you're wanted over here.'

The first-grader came over to me and I said,
'Turn around.'

The first-grader turned around and I wrote
'Trout fishing in America' on his back. It
looked even better on the second first-grader.
We couldn't help but admire it. 'Trout fishing
in America'. It certainly did add something to
the first-graders. It completed them and
gave them a kind of class.

'It really looks good, doesn't it?'

'Yeah.'

'Let's get some more chalk.'

'Sure.'

'There are a lot of first-graders over there
by the monkey-bars.'

'Yeah.'

We all got hold of chalk and later in the day,
by the end of lunch period, almost all of the
first-graders had 'Trout fishing in America'
written on their backs, girls included.

Complaints began arriving at the principal's
office from the first-grade teachers. One of the
complaints was in the form of a little girl.

'Miss Robins sent me,' she said to the
principal. 'She told me to have you look at
this.'

'Look at what?' the principal said, staring at
the empty child.

'At my back,' she said.

The little girl turned around and the
principal read aloud, 'Trout fishing in
America.'

'Who did this?' the principal said.

'That gang of sixth-graders,' she said. 'The
bad ones. They've done it to all us first-
graders. We all look like this. ''Trout fishing
in America.'' What does it mean? I just got this
sweater new from my grandma.'

'Huh. ''Trout fishing in America'',' the
principal said. 'Tell Miss Robins I'll be down
to see her in a little while,' and excused the
girl and a short time later we terrorists
were summoned up from the lower world.

We reluctantly stamped into the principal's
office, fidgeting and pawing our feet and
looking out the windows and yawning and one of
us suddenly got an insane blink going and
putting our hands into our pockets and looking
away and then back again and looking up at the
light fixture on the ceiling, how much it
looked like a boiled potato, and down again
and at the picture of the principal's mother
on the wall. She had been a star in the silent
pictures and was tied to a railroad track.

'Does ''Trout fishing in America'' seem at all
familiar to you boys?' the principal said. 'I
wonder if perhaps you've seen it written down
anywhere today in your travels? ''Trout fishing
in America.'' Think hard about it for a minute.'

We all thought hard about it.

There was a silence in the room, a silence

that we all knew intimately, having been at
the principal's office quite a few times in the
past.

'Let me see if I can help you,' the principal
said. 'Perhaps you saw "Trout fishing in
America" written in chalk on the backs of
the first-graders. I wonder how it got there.'

We couldn't help but smile nervously.

'I just came back from Miss Robins's first-
grade class,' the principal said. 'I asked all
those who had ''Trout fishing in America''
written on their backs to hold up their hands,
and all the children in the class held up their
hands, except one and he had spent his whole
lunch period hiding in the lavatory. What do you
boys make of it ...? This ''Trout fishing in
America'' business?'

We didn't say anything.

The one of us still had his mad blink going. I
am certain that it was his guilty blink that
always gave us away. We should have gotten rid
of him at the beginning of the sixth grade.

'You're all guilty, aren't you?' he said. 'Is
there one of you who isn't guilty? If there is,
speak up. Now.'

We were all silent except for blink, blink,
blink, blink, blink. Suddenly I could <u>hear</u>
his God-damn eye blinking. It was very much like
the sound of an insect laying the 1,000,000th
egg of our disaster.

'The whole bunch of you did it. Why? ... Why
''Trout fishing in America'' on the backs of
the first-graders?'

And then the principal went into his famous
$E=MC^2$ sixth-grade gimmick, the thing he always
used in dealing with us.

'Now wouldn't it look funny,' he said. 'If I
asked all your teachers to come in here, and

51

then I told the teachers all to turn around, and then I took a piece of chalk and wrote "Trout fishing in America" on their backs?'

We all giggled nervously and blushed faintly.

'Would you like to see your teachers walking around all day with "Trout fishing in America" written on their backs, trying to teach you about Cuba? That would look silly, wouldn't it? You wouldn't like to see that, would you? That wouldn't do at all, would it?'

'No,' we said like a Greek chorus, some of us saying it with our voices and some of us by nodding our heads, and then there was the blink, blink, blink.

'That's what I thought,' he said. 'The first-graders look up to you and admire you like the teachers look up to me and admire me. It just won't do to write "Trout fishing in America" on their backs. Are we agreed, gentlemen?'

We were agreed.

I tell you it worked every God-damn time.

Of course it had to work.

'All right,' he said. 'I'll consider trout fishing in America to have come to an end. Agreed?'

'Agreed.'

'Agreed?'

'Agreed.'

'Blink, blink.'

But it wasn't completely over, for it took a while to get trout fishing in America off the clothes of the first-graders. A fair percentage of trout fishing in America was gone the next day. The mothers did this by simply putting clean clothes on their children, but there were a lot of kids whose mothers just tried to wipe it off and then sent them back to school the next day with the same clothes on, but you could still see 'Trout fishing in America' faintly outlined on their backs. But after a few more days trout fishing in America disappeared altogether as it was destined to from its very beginning, and a kind of autumn fell over the first grade.

TROUT FISHING IN AMERICA WITH THE FBI

Dear Trout Fishing in America,

   last week walking along lower market on the
way to work saw the pictures of the FBI's TEN
MOST WANTED MEN in the window of a store. the
dodger under one of the pictures was folded
under at both sides and you couldn't read all of
it. the picture showed a nice, clean-cut-looking
guy with freckles and curly (red?) hair

                        WANTED FOR:
              RICHARD LAWRENCE MARQUETTE
   Aliases: Richard Lawrence Marquette, Richard
            Lourence Marquette
   Description:
26, born Dec. 12, 1934, Portland, Oregon
170 to 180 pounds
muscular
light brown, cut short
blue
   Complexion: ruddy
   Race: white

        Nationality: American
        Occupations: auto body w
                                                  recapper, s
                                                  survey rod
arks: 6″ hernia scar; tattoo 'Mom' in wreath on
ight forearm
ull upper denture, may also have lower denture.
                         Reportedly frequents
s, and is an avid trout fisherman.

(this is how the dodger looked cut off on both
sides and you couldn't make out any more, even
what he was wanted for.)

                         Your old buddy,

                              Pard

Dear Pard,

   Your letter explains why I saw two FBI agents
watching a trout stream last week. They watched
a path that came down through the trees and
then circled a large black stump and led to
a deep pool. Trout were rising in the pool.
The FBI agents watched the path, the trees, the
black stump, the pool and the trout as if they
were all holes punched in a card that had just
come out of a computer. The afternoon sun kept
changing everything as it moved across the sky,
and the FBI agents kept changing with the
sun. It appears to be part of their training.

                         Your friend,

                         Trout Fishing in America

WORSEWICK

Worsewick Hot Springs was nothing fancy.
Somebody put some boards across the creek.
That was it.
  The boards dammed up the creek enough to form
a huge bathtub there, and the creek flowed over
the top of the boards, invited like a postcard
to the ocean a thousand miles away.
  As I said Worsewick was nothing fancy, not
like the places where the swells go. There were
no buildings around. We saw an old shoe lying by
the tub.
  The hot springs came down off a hill and where
they flowed there was a bright orange scum
through the sagebrush. The hot springs flowed
into the creek right there at the tub and that's
where it was nice.
  We parked our car on the dirt road and went
down and took off our clothes, then we took off
the baby's clothes, and the deerflies had at
us until we got into the water, and then they
stopped.
  There was a green slime growing around the

edges of the tub and there were dozens of dead
fish floating in our bath. Their bodies had
been turned white by death, like frost on iron
doors. Their eyes were large and stiff.

The fish had made the mistake of going down
the creek too far and ending up in hot water
singing, 'When you lose your money, learn to
lose.'

We played and relaxed in the water. The green
slime and the dead fish played and relaxed
with us and flowed out over us and entwined
themselves about us.

Splashing around in that hot water with my
woman, I began to get ideas, as they say. After
a while I placed my body in such a position
in the water that the baby could not see my
hard-on.

I did this by going deeper and deeper in the
water, like a dinosaur, and letting the green
slime and dead fish cover me over.

My woman took the baby out of the water and
gave her a bottle and put her back in the car.
The baby was tired. It was really time for her
to take a nap.

My woman took a blanket out of the car and
covered up the windows that faced the hot
springs. She put the blanket on top of the car
and then lay rocks on the blanket to hold it in
place. I remember her standing there by the car.

Then she came back to the water, and the
deerflies were at her, and then it was my turn.
After a while she said, 'I don't have my
diaphragm with me and besides it wouldn't work
in the water, anyway. I think it's a good idea
if you don't come inside me. What do you think?

I thought this over and said all right. I
didn't want any more kids for a long time.
The green slime and dead fish were all

57

about our bodies.

I remember a dead fish floated under her neck. I waited for it to come up on the other side, and it came up on the other side.

Worsewick was nothing fancy.

Then I came, and just cleared her in a split second like an aeroplane in the movies, pulling out of a nosedive and sailing over the roof of a school.

My sperm came out into the water, unaccustomed to the light, and instantly it became a misty, stringy kind of thing and swirled out like a falling star, and I saw a dead fish come forward and float into my sperm, bending it in the middle. His eyes were stiff like iron.

THE SHIPPING OF TROUT FISHING IN AMERICA
SHORTY TO NELSON ALGREN

Trout Fishing in America Shorty appeared
suddenly last autumn in San Francisco,
staggering around in a magnificent chrome-plated
steel wheelchair.

He was a legless, screaming middle-aged wino.

He descended upon North Beach like a chapter
from the Old Testament. He was the reason birds
migrate in the autumn. They have to. He was the
cold turning of the earth; the bad wind that
blows off sugar.

He would stop children on the street and say
to them, 'I ain't got no legs. The trout chopped
my legs off in Fort Lauderdale. You kids got
legs. The trout didn't chop your legs off.
Wheel me into that store over there.'

The kids, frightened and embarrassed, would
wheel Trout Fishing in America Shorty into the
store. It would always be a store that sold
sweet wine, and he would buy a bottle of wine
and then he'd have the kids wheel him back out
on to the street, and he would open the wine and
start drinking there on the street just like he

was Winston Churchill.

After a while the children would run and hide when they saw Trout Fishing in America Shorty coming.

'I pushed him last week,'

'I pushed him yesterday,'

'Quick, let's hide behind these garbage cans.'

And they would hide behind the garbage cans while Trout Fishing in America Shorty staggered by in his wheelchair. The kids would hold their breath until he was gone.

Trout Fishing in America Shorty used to go down to L'Italia, the Italian newspaper in North Beach at Stockton and Green Streets. Old Italians gather in front of the newspaper in the afternoon and just stand there, leaning up against the building, talking and dying in the sun.

Trout Fishing in America Shorty used to wheel into the middle of them as if they were a bunch of pigeons, bottle of wine in hand, and begin shouting obscenities in fake Italian.

Tra-la-la-la-la-la- Spa-ghet-tiii!

I remember Trout Fishing in America Shorty passed out in Washington Square, right in front of the Benjamin Franklin statue. He had fallen face first out of his wheelchair and just lay there without moving.

Snoring loudly.

Above him were the metal works of Benjamin Franklin like a clock, hat in hand.

Trout Fishing in America Shorty lay there below, his face spread out like a fan in the grass.

A friend and I got to talking about Trout Fishing in America Shorty one afternoon. We decided the best thing to do with him was to pack him in a big shipping crate with a couple

of cases of sweet wine and send him to Nelson
Algren.

Nelson Algren is always writing about Railroad
Shorty, a hero of the Neon Wilderness (the
reason for 'The Face on the Barroom Floor')
and the destroyer of Dove Linkhorn in A Walk on
the Wild Side.

We thought that Nelson Algren would make the
perfect custodian for Trout Fishing in
America Shorty. Maybe a museum might be started.
Trout Fishing in America Shorty could be the
first piece in an important collection.

We would nail him up in a packing crate with
a big label on it.

        Contents:
        Trout Fishing in America Shorty

        Occupation:
        Wino

        Address:
        C/O Nelson Algren
        Chicago

And there would be stickers all over the
crate, saying: 'GLASS/HANDLE WITH CARE/SPECIAL
HANDLING/GLASS/DON'T SPILL/THIS SIDE UP/HANDLE
THIS WINO LIKE HE WAS AN ANGEL'

And Trout Fishing in America Shorty,
grumbling, puking and cursing in his crate
would travel across America, from San Francisco
to Chicago.

And Trout Fishing in America Shorty, wondering
what it was all about, would travel on,
shouting 'Where in the hell am I? I can't see to
open this bottle! Who turned out the lights?

Fuck this motel! I have to take a piss!
Where's my key?'

It was a good idea.

A few days after we made our plans for Trout
Fishing in America Shorty, a heavy rain was
pouring down upon San Francisco. The rain
turned the streets inwards, like drowned lungs,
upon themselves and I was hurrying to work,
meeting swollen gutters at the intersections.

I saw Trout Fishing in America Shorty passed
out in the front window of a Filipino
laundromat. He was sitting in his wheelchair
with closed eyes staring out of the window.

There was a tranquil expression on his face.
He almost looked human. He had probably fallen
asleep while he was having his brains washed in
one of the machines.

Weeks passed and we never got around to
shipping Trout Fishing in America Shorty away
to Nelson Algren. We kept putting it off. One
thing and another. Then we lost our golden
opportunity because Trout Fishing in America
Shorty disappeared a little while after
that.

They probably swept him up one morning and put
him in jail to punish him, the evil fart, or
they put him in a nut-house to dry him out a
little.

Maybe Trout Fishing in America Shorty just
pedalled down to San Jose in his wheelchair,
rattling along the freeway at a quarter of a
mile an hour.

I don't know what happened to him. But if he
comes back to San Francisco someday and dies,
I have an idea.

Trout Fishing in America Shorty should be
buried right beside the Benjamin Franklin statue
in Washington Square. We should anchor his

wheelchair to a huge grey stone and write upon
the stone:

> Trout Fishing in America Shorty
> 20¢ Wash
> 10¢ Dry
> Forever

THE MAYOR OF THE TWENTIETH CENTURY

London. On December 1, 1887; July 7, August 8,
September 30, one day in the month of October
and on the 9th of November, 1888; on the 1st of
June, the 17th of July and the 10th of
September 1889 ...

The disguise was perfect.

Nobody ever saw him, except, of course, the
victims. They saw him.

Who would have expected?

He wore a costume of trout fishing in America.
He wore mountains on his elbows and bluejays
on the collar of his shirt. Deep water flowed
through the lilies that were entwined about
his shoelaces. A bullfrog kept croaking in his
watch pocket and the air was filled with the
sweet smell of ripe blackberry bushes.

He wore trout fishing in America as a costume
to hide his own appearance from the world while
he performed his deeds of murder in the night.

Who would have expected?

Nobody!

Scotland Yard?

(Pouf!)
They were always a hundred miles away,
wearing halibut-stalker hats, looking under
the dust.

Nobody ever found out.

O, now he's the Mayor of the Twentieth
Century! A razor, a knife and a ukelele are his
favourite instruments.

Of course, it would have to be a ukelele.
Nobody else would have thought of it, pulled
like a plough through the intestines.

ON PARADISE

'Speaking of evacuations, your missive, while
complete in other regards, skirted the subject,
though you did deal briefly with rural
micturition procedure. I consider this a gross
oversight on your part, as I'm certain you're
well aware of my unending fascination with
camp-out crapping. Please rush details in your
next effort. Slit-trench, pith helmet,
slingshot, biffy and if so number of holes and
proximity of keester to vermin and deposits of
prior users.'

                              - From a Letter by a Friend

   Sheep. Everything smelled of sheep on Paradise
Creek, but there were no sheep in sight. I
fished down from the ranger station where there
was a huge monument to the Civilian Conservation
Corps.
   It was a twelve-foot high marble statue of a
young man walking out on a cold morning to a
crapper that had the classic half-moon cut
above the door.

The 1930s will never come again, but his shoes were wet with dew. They'll stay that way in marble.

I went off into the marsh. There the creek was soft and spread out in the grass like a beer belly. The fishing was difficult. Summer ducks were jumping up into flight. They were big mallards with their Rainier Ale-like offspring.

I believe I saw a woodcock. He had a long bill like putting a fire hydrant into a pencil sharpener, then pasting it on to a bird and letting the bird fly away in front of me with this thing on its face for no other purpose than to amaze me.

I worked my way slowly out of the marsh until the creek again became a muscular thing, the strongest Paradise Creek in the world. I was then close enough to see the sheep. There were hundreds of them.

Everything smelled of sheep. The dandelions were suddenly more sheep than flower, each petal reflecting wool and the sound of a bell ringing off the yellow. But the thing that smelled the most like sheep, was the very sun itself. When the sun went behind a cloud, the smell of the sheep decreased, like standing on some old guy's hearing aid, and when the sun came back again, the smell of the sheep was loud, like a clap of thunder inside a cup of coffee.

That afternoon the sheep crossed the creek in front of my hook. They were so close that their shadows fell across my bait. I practically caught trout up their assholes.

THE CABINET OF DOCTOR CALIGARI

Once water bugs were my field. I remember that
childhood spring when I studied the winter-long
mud puddles of the Pacific North-west. I had a
fellowship.

My books were a pair of Sears Roebuck boots,
ones with green rubber pages. Most of my
classrooms were close to the shore. That's
where the important things were happening and
that's where the good things were happening.

Sometimes as experiments I laid boards out
into the mud puddles, so I could look into the
deeper water but it was not nearly as good as
the water in close to the shore.

The water bugs were so small I practically had
to lay my vision like a drowned orange on the
mud puddle. There is a romance about fruit
floating outside on the water, about apples and
pears in rivers and lakes. For the first minute
or so, I saw nothing, and then slowly the water
bugs came into being.

I saw a black one with big teeth chasing a
white one with a bag of newspapers slung over

its shoulder, two white ones playing cards near
the window, a fourth white one staring back
with a harmonica in its mouth.

I was a scholar until the mud puddles went
dry and then I picked cherries for two-and-a-
half cents a pound in an old orchard that
was beside a long, hot dusty road.

The cherry boss was a middle-aged woman who
was a real Okie. Wearing a pair of goofy
overalls, her name was Rebel Smith, and she'd
been a friend of 'Pretty Boy' Floyd's down in
Oklahoma. 'I remember one afternoon "Pretty
Boy" came driving up in his car. I ran out on
to the front porch.'

Rebel Smith was always smoking cigarettes and
showing people how to pick cherries and
assigning them to trees and writing down
everything in a little book she carried in her
shirt pocket. She smoked just half a cigarette
and then threw the other half on the ground.

For the first few days of the picking, I was
always seeing her half-smoked cigarettes lying
all over the orchard, near the john and around
the trees and down the rows.

Then she hired half-a-dozen bums to pick
cherries because the picking was going too
slowly. Rebel picked the bums up on skidrow
every morning and drove them out to the orchard
in a rusty old truck. There were always
half-a-dozen bums, but sometimes they had
different faces.

After they came to pick cherries I never saw
any more of her half-smoked cigarettes lying
around. They were gone before they hit the
ground. Looking back on it, you might say that
Rebel Smith was anti-mud puddle, but then you
might not say that at all.

THE SALT CREEK COYOTES

High and lonesome and steady, it's the smell of
sheep down in the valley that has done it to
them. Here all afternoon in the rain I've been
listening to the sound of the coyotes up on
Salt Creek.

The smell of the sheep grazing in the valley
has done it to them. Their voices water and
come down the canyon, past the summer homes.
Their voices are a creek, running down the
mountain, over the bones of sheep, living and
dead.

O, THERE ARE COYOTES UP ON SALT CREEK so the
sign on the trail says, and it also says,
WATCH OUT FOR CYANIDE CAPSULES PUT ALONG THE
CREEK TO KILL COYOTES. DON'T PICK THEM UP AND
EAT THEM: NOT UNLESS YOU'RE A COYOTE. THEY'LL
KILL YOU. LEAVE THEM ALONE.

Then the sign says this all over again in
Spanish. ¡AH! HAY COYOTES EN SALT CREEK,
TAMBIEN. CUIDADO CON LAS CAPSULAS DE CIANURO:
MATAN. NO LAS COMA; A MENOS QUE SEA VD. UN
COYOTE. MATAN. NO LAS TOQUE.

It does not say it in Russian.

I asked an old guy in a bar about those cyanide capsules up on Salt Creek and he told me that they were a kind of pistol. They put a pleasing coyote scent on the trigger (probably the smell of a coyote snatch) and then a coyote comes along and gives it a good sniff, a fast feel and BLAM! That's all, brother.

I went fishing up on Salt Creek and caught a nice little Dolly Varden trout, spotted and slender as a snake you'd expect to find in a jewellery store, but after a while I could think only of the gas chamber at San Quentin.

O Caryl Chessman and Alexander Robillard Vistas! as if they were names for tracts of three-bedroom houses with wall-to-wall carpets and plumbing that defies the imagination.

Then it came to me up there on Salt Creek, capital punishment being what it is, an act of state business with no song down the railroad track after the train has gone and no vibration on the rails, that they should take the head of a coyote killed by one of those God-damn cyanide things up on Salt Creek and hollow it out and dry it in the sun and then make it into a crown with the teeth running in a circle around the top of it and a nice green light coming off the teeth.

Then the witnesses and newspapermen and gas chamber flunkies would have to watch a king wearing a coyote crown die there in front of them, the gas rising in the chamber like a rain mist drifting down the mountain from Salt Creek. It has been raining here now for two days, and through the trees, the heart stops beating.

THE HUNCHBACK TROUT

The creek was made narrow by little green trees
that grew too close together. The creek was like
12,845 telephone booths in a row with high
Victorian ceilings and all the doors taken off
and all the backs of the booths knocked out.

Sometimes when I went fishing in there, I felt
just like a telephone repairman, even though I
did not look like one. I was only a kid covered
with fishing tackle, but in some strange way by
going in there and catching a few trout, I kept
the telephones in service. I was an asset to
society.

It was pleasant work, but at times it made me
uneasy. It could grow dark in there instantly
when there were some clouds in the sky and they
worked their way on to the sun. Then you almost
needed candles to fish by, and foxfire in your
reflexes.

Once I was in there when it started raining.
It was dark and hot and steamy. I was of course
on overtime. I had that going in my favour. I
caught seven trout in fifteen minutes.

The trout in those telephone booths were good
fellows. There were a lot of young cutthroat
trout six to nine inches long, perfect pan size
for local calls. Sometimes there were a few
fellows, eleven inches or so – for the long
distance calls.

I've always liked cutthroat trout. They put
up a good fight, running against the bottom and
then broad jumping. Under their throats they fly
the orange banner of Jack the Ripper.

Also in the creek were a few stubborn rainbow
trout, seldom heard from, but there all the
same, like certified public accountants. I'd
catch one every once in a while. They were fat
and chunky, almost as wide as they were long.
I've heard those trout called 'squire' trout.

It used to take me about an hour to hitchhike
to that creek. There was a river nearby. The
river wasn't much. The creek was where I
punched in. Leaving my card above the clock,
I'd punch out again when it was time to go home.

I remember the afternoon I caught the
hunchback trout.

A farmer gave me a ride in a truck. He picked
me up at a traffic signal beside a bean field
and he never said a word to me.

His stopping and picking me up and driving me
down the road was as automatic a thing to him as
closing the barn door, nothing need be said
about it, but still I was in motion travelling
thirty-five miles an hour down the road,
watching houses and groves of trees go by,
watching chickens and mailboxes enter and pass
through my vision.

Then I did not see any houses for a while.
'This is where I get out,' I said.

The farmer nodded his head. The truck stopped.
'Thanks a lot,' I said.

73

The farmer did not ruin his audition for the Metropolitan Opera by making a sound. He just nodded his head again. The truck started up. He was the original silent old farmer.

A little while later I was punching in at the creek. I put my card above the clock and went into that long tunnel of telephone booths.

I waded about seventy-three telephone booths in. I caught two trout in a little hole that was like a wagon wheel. It was one of my favourite holes, and always good for a trout or two.

I always like to think of that hole as a kind of pencil sharpener. I put my reflexes in and they came back out with a good point on them. Over a period of a couple of years, I must have caught fifty trout in that hole, though it was only as big as a wagon wheel.

I was fishing with salmon eggs and using a size 14 single egg hook on a pound and a quarter test tippet. The two trout lay in my creel covered entirely by green ferns, ferns made gentle and fragile by the damp walls of telephone booths.

The next good place was forty-five telephone booths in. The place was at the end of a run of gravel, brown and slippery with algae. The run of gravel dropped off and disappeared at a little shelf where there were some white rocks.

One of the rocks was kind of strange. It was a flat white rock. Off by itself from the other rocks, it reminded me of a white cat I had seen in my childhood.

The cat had fallen or been thrown off a high wooden sidewalk that went along the side of a hill in Tacoma, Washington. The cat was lying in a parking lot below.

The fall had not appreciably helped the thickness of the cat, and then a few people had

74

parked their cars on the cat. Of course, that
was a long time ago and the cars looked
different from the way they look now.

You hardly see those cars any more. They are
the old cars. They have to get off the highway
because they can't keep up.

That flat white rock off by itself from the
other rocks reminded me of that dead cat come to
lie there in the creek, among 12,845 telephone
booths.

I threw out a salmon egg and let it drift
down over that rock and WHAM! a good hit! and I
had the fish on and it ran hard downstream,
cutting at an angle and staying deep and really
coming on hard, solid and uncompromising, and
then the fish jumped and for a second I thought
it was a frog. I'd never seen a fish like that
before.

God-damn! What the hell!

The fish ran deep again and I could feel its
life energy screaming back up the line to my
hand. The line felt like sound. It was like an
ambulance siren coming straight at me, red light
flashing, and then going away again and then
taking to the air and becoming an air-raid
siren.

The fish jumped a few more times and it still
looked like a frog, but it didn't have any legs.
Then the fish grew tired and sloppy, and I
swung and splashed it up the surface of the
creek and into my net.

The fish was a twelve-inch rainbow trout with
a huge hump on its back. A hunchback trout.
The first I'd ever seen. The hump was probably
due to an injury that occurred when the trout
was young. Maybe a horse stepped on it or a tree
fell over in a storm or its mother spawned
where they were building a bridge.

There was a fine thing about that trout. I only wish I could have made a death mask of him. Not of his body though, but of his energy. I don't know if anyone would have understood his body. I put it in my creel.

Later in the afternoon when the telephone booths began to grow dark at the edges, I punched out of the creek and went home. I had that hunchback trout for dinner. Wrapped in cornmeal and fried in butter, its hump tasted sweet as the kisses of Esmeralda.

THE TEDDY ROOSEVELT CHINGADER'

The Challis National Forest was created July 1, 1908, by Executive Order of President Theodore Roosevelt ... Twenty Million years ago, scientists tell us, three-toed horses, camels, and possibly rhinoceroses were plentiful in this section of the country.

This is part of my history in the Challis National Forest. We came over through Lowman after spending a little time with my woman's Mormon relatives at McCall, where we learned about Spirit Prison and couldn't find Duck Lake.

I carried the baby up the mountain. The sign said 1½ miles. There was a green sports car parked on the road. We walked up the trail until we met a man with a green sports car hat on and a girl in a light summer dress.

She had her dress rolled above her knees and when she saw us coming, she rolled her dress down. The man had a bottle of wine in his back pocket. The wine was in a long green bottle. It looked funny sticking out of his back pocket.

'How far is it to Spirit Prison?' I asked.

'You're about halfway,' he said.

The girl smiled. She had blonde hair and they went on down. Bounce, bounce, bounce, like a pair of birthday balls, down through the trees and boulders.

I put the baby down in a patch of snow lying in the hollow behind a big stump. She played in the snow and then started eating it. I remembered something from a book by Justice of the Supreme Court, William O. Douglas. DON'T EAT SNOW. IT'S BAD FOR YOU AND WILL GIVE YOU A STOMACH ACHE.

'Stop eating that snow!' I said to the baby.

I put her on my shoulders and continued up the path towards Spirit Prison. That's where everybody who isn't a Mormon goes when they die. All Catholics, Buddhists, Moslems, Jews, Baptists, Methodists and International Jewel Thieves. Everybody who isn't a Mormon goes to the Spirit Slammer.

The sign said 1½ miles. The path was easy to follow, then it just stopped. We lost it near a creek. I looked all around. I looked on both sides of the creek, but the path had just vanished.

Could be the fact that we were still alive had something to do with it. Hard to tell.

We turned around and started back down the mountain. The baby cried when she saw the snow again, holding out her hands for the snow. We didn't have time to stop. It was getting late.

We got in our car and drove back to McCall. That evening we talked about Communism. The Mormon girl read aloud to us from a book called <u>The Naked Communist</u> written by an ex-police chief of Salt Lake City.

My woman asked the girl if she believed the book were written under the influence of Divine Power, if she considered the book to be a religious text of some sort.

The girl said, 'No.'

I bought a pair of tennis shoes and three pairs of socks at a store in McCall. The socks had a written guarantee. I tried to save the guarantee, but I put it in my pocket and lost it. The guarantee said that if anything happened to the socks within three months time, I would get new socks. It seemed like a good idea.

I was supposed to launder the old socks and send them in with the guarantee. Right off the bat, new socks would be on their way, travelling across America with my name on the package. Then all I would have to do, would be to open the package, take those new socks out and put them on. They would look good on my feet.

I wish I hadn't lost that guarantee. That was a shame. I've had to face the fact that new socks are not going to be a family heirloom. Losing the guarantee took care of that. All future generations are on their own.

We left McCall the next day, the day after I lost the sock guarantee, following the muddy water of the North Fork of the Payette down and the clear water of the South Fork up.

We stopped at Lowman and had a strawberry milkshake and then drove back into the mountains along Clear Creek and over the summit to Bear Creek.

There were signs nailed to the trees all along Bear Creek, the signs said, 'IF YOU FISH IN THIS CREEK, WE'LL HIT YOU IN THE HEAD.' I didn't

want to be hit in the head, so I kept my
fishing tackle right there in the car.

We saw a flock of sheep. There's a sound that
the baby makes when she sees furry animals.
She also makes that sound when she sees her
mother and me naked. She made that sound and we
drove out of the sheep like an aeroplane flies
out of the clouds.

We entered Challis National Forest about five
miles away from that sound. Driving now along
Valley Creek, we saw the Sawtooth Mountains for
the first time. It was clouding over and we
thought it was going to rain.

'Looks like it's raining in Stanley,' I said,
though I had never been in Stanley before. It
is easy to say things about Stanley when you
have never been there. We saw the road to
Bull Trout Lake. The road looked good. When we
reached Stanley, the streets were white and
dry like a collision at a high rate of speed
between a cemetery and a truck loaded with sacks
of flour.

We stopped at a store in Stanley. I bought a
candy bar and asked how the trout fishing was
in Cuba. The woman at the store said, 'You're
better off dead, you Commie bastard.' I got
a receipt for the candy bar to be used for
income tax purposes.

The old ten-cent deduction.

I didn't learn anything about fishing in that
store. The people were awfully nervous,
especially a young man who was folding overalls.
He had about a hundred pairs left to fold and
he was really nervous.

We went over to a restaurant and I had a
hamburger and my woman had a cheeseburger and
the baby ran in circles like a bat at the
World's Fair.

There was a girl there in her early teens or
maybe she was only ten years old. She wore
lipstick and had a loud voice and seemed to be
aware of boys. She got a lot of fun out of
sweeping the front porch of the restaurant.

She came in and played around with the baby.
She was very good with the baby. Her voice
dropped down and got soft with the baby. She
told us that her father'd had a heart attack and
was still in bed. 'He can't get up and around,'
she said.

We had some more coffee and I thought about
the Mormons. That very morning we had said
goodbye to them, after having drunk coffee
in their house.

The smell of coffee had been like a spider web
in the house. It had not been an easy smell. It
had not lent itself to religious contemplation,
thoughts of temple work to be done in Salt Lake,
dead relatives to be discovered among ancient
papers in Illinois and Germany. Then more
temple work to be done in Salt Lake.

The Mormon woman told us that when she had
been married in the temple at Salt Lake, a
mosquito had bitten her on the wrist just before
the ceremony and her wrist had swollen up and
become huge and just awful. It could've been
seen through the lace by a blind man. She had
been so embarrassed.

She told us that those Salt Lake mosquitoes
always made her swell up when they bit her. Last
year, she had told us, she'd been in Salt Lake,
doing some temple work for a dead relative
when a mosquito had bitten her and her whole
body had swollen up. 'I felt so embarrassed,'
she had told us. 'Walking around like a
balloon.'

We finished our coffee and left. Not a drop of

81

rain had fallen in Stanley. It was about an
hour before sundown.

We drove up to Big Redfish Lake, about four
miles from Stanley and looked it over. Big
Redfish Lake is the Forest Lawn of camping in
Idaho, laid out for maximum comfort. There
were a lot of people camped there, and some of
them looked as if they had been camped there for
a long time.

We decided that we were too young to camp at
Big Redfish Lake, and besides they charged fifty
cents a day, three dollars a week like a
skidrow hotel, and there were just too many
people there. There were too many trailers and
campers parked in the halls. We couldn't get
to the elevator because there was a family
from New York parked there in a ten-room
trailer.

Three children came by drinking rub-a-dub and
pulling an old granny by her legs. Her legs were
straight out and stiff and her butt was banging
on the carpet. Those kids were pretty drunk
and the old granny wasn't too sober either,
shouting something like, 'Let the Civil War
come again, I'm ready to fuck!'

We went down to Little Redfish Lake. The
campgrounds there were just about abandoned.
There were so many people up at Big Redfish Lake
and practically nobody camping at Little
Redfish Lake, and it was free, too.

We wondered what was wrong with the camp. If
perhaps a camping plague, a sure destroyer that
leaves all your camping equipment, your car and
your sex organs in tatters like old sails,
had swept the camp just a few days before, and
those few people who were staying at the camp
now, were staying there because they didn't have
any sense.

We joined them enthusiastically. The camp had
a beautiful view of the mountains. We found a
place that really looked good, right on the
lake.

Unit 4 had a stove. It was a square metal box
mounted on a cement block. There was a stove
pipe on top of the box, but there were no bullet
holes in the pipe. I was amazed. Almost all the
camp stoves we had seen in Idaho had been full
of bullet holes. I guess it's only reasonable
that people, when they get the chance, would
want to shoot some old stove sitting in the
woods.

Unit 4 had a big wooden table with benches
attached to it like a pair of those old
Benjamin Franklin glasses, the ones with those
funny square lenses. I sat down on the left
lens, facing the Sawtooth Mountains. Like
astigmatism, I made myself at home.

FOOTNOTE CHAPTER TO 'THE SHIPPING OF TROUT FISHING IN AMERICA SHORTY TO NELSON ALGREN'

Well, well, Trout Fishing in America Shorty's back in town, but I don't think it's going to be the same as it was before. Those good old days are over because Trout Fishing in America Shorty is famous. The movies have discovered him.

Last week 'The New Wave' took him out of his wheelchair and laid him out in a cobblestone alley. Then they shot some footage of him. He ranted and raved and they put it down on film.

Later on, probably, a different voice will be dubbed in. It will be a noble and eloquent voice denouncing man's inhumanity to man in no uncertain terms.

'Trout Fishing in America Shorty, Mon Amour.'

His soliloquy beginning with, 'I was once a famous skip-tracer known throughout America as "Grasshopper Nijinsky". Nothing was too good for me. Beautiful blondes followed me wherever I went.' Etc ... They'll milk it for all it's worth and make cream and butter from a pair of empty pants legs and a low budget.

But I may be all wrong. What was being shot
may have been just a scene from a new science-
fiction movie 'Trout Fishing in America Shorty
from Outer Space'. One of those cheap thrillers
with the theme: Scientists, mad-or-otherwise,
should never play God, that ends with the castle
on fire and a lot of people walking home
through the dark woods.

THE PUDDING MASTER OF STANLEY BASIN

Tree, snow and rock beginnings, the mountain in
back of the lake promised us eternity, but the
lake itself was filled with thousands of silly
minnows, swimming close to the shore and busy
putting in hours of Mack Sennett time.

The minnows were an Idaho tourist attraction.
They should have been made into a National
Monument. Swimming close to shore, like
children, they believed in their own
immortality.

A third-year student in engineering at the
University of Montana attempted to catch some of
the minnows but he went about it all wrong.
So did the children who came on the Fourth of
July weekend.

The children waded out into the lake and tried
to catch the minnows with their hands. They
also used milk cartons and plastic bags. They
presented the lake with hours of human effort.
Their total catch was one minnow. It jumped
out of a can full of water on their table and
died under the table, gasping for watery breath

while their mother fried eggs on the Coleman
stove.

The mother apologized. She was supposed to be
watching the fish - THIS IS MY EARTHLY FAILURE -
holding the dead fish by the tail, the fish
taking all the bows like a young Jewish
comedian talking about Adlai Stevenson.

The third-year student in engineering at the
University of Montana took a tin can and
punched an elaborate design of holes in the can,
the design running around and around in circles,
like a dog with a fire hydrant in its mouth.
Then he attached some string to the can and put
a huge salmon egg and a piece of Swiss cheese
in the can. After two hours of intimate and
universal failure, he went back to Missoula,
Montana.

The woman who travels with me discovered the
best way to catch the minnows. She used a large
pan that had in its bottom the dregs of a
distant vanilla pudding. She put the pan in the
shallow water along the shore and instantly,
hundreds of minnows gathered around. Then,
mesmerized by the vanilla pudding, they swam
like a children's crusade into the pan. She
caught twenty fish with one dip. She put the
pan full of fish on the shore and the baby
played with the fish for an hour.

We watched the baby to make sure she was just
leaning on them a little. We didn't want her to
kill any of them because she was too young.

Instead of making her furry sound, she
adapted rapidly to the difference between
animals and fish, and was soon making a silver
sound.

She caught one of the fish with her hand and
looked at it for a while. We took the fish out
of her hand and put it back into the pan.

After a while she was putting the fish back by
herself.

Then she grew tired of this. She tipped the
pan over and a dozen fish flopped out on to the
shore. The children's game and the banker's
game, she picked up those silver things, one at
a time, and put them back in the pan. There
was still a little water in it. The fish liked
this. You could tell.

When she got tired of the fish, we put them
back in the lake, and they were all quite alive,
but nervous. I doubt if they will ever want
vanilla pudding again.

ROOM 208, HOTEL TROUT FISHING IN AMERICA

Half a block from Broadway and Columbus is Hotel
Trout Fishing in America, a cheap hotel. It
is very old and run by some Chinese. They are
young and ambitious Chinese and the lobby is
filled with the smell of Lysol.

The Lysol sits like another guest on the
stuffed furniture, reading a copy of the
Chronicle, the Sports Section. It is the only
furniture I have ever seen in my life that looks
like baby food.

And the Lysol sits asleep next to an old
Italian pensioner who listens to the heavy
ticking of the clock and dreams of eternity's
golden pasta, sweet basil and Jesus Christ.

The Chinese are always doing something to the
hotel. One week they paint a lower banister and
the next week they put some new wallpaper on
part of the third floor.

No matter how many times you pass that part of
the third floor, you cannot remember the
colour of the wallpaper or what the design is.
All you know is that part of the wallpaper is

new. It is different from the old wallpaper.
But you cannot remember what that looks like
either.

One day the Chinese take a bed out of a room
and lean it up against the wall. It stays there
for a month. You get used to seeing it and then
you go by one day and it is gone. You wonder
where it went.

I remember the first time I went inside Hotel
Trout Fishing in America. It was with a friend
to meet some people.

'I'll tell you what's happening,' he said.
'She's an ex-hustler who works for the telephone
company. He went to medical school for a while
during the Great Depression and then he went
into show business. After that, he was an errand
boy for an abortion mill in Los Angeles. He
took a fall and did some time in San Quentin.

'I think you'll like them. They're good people.

'He met her a couple of years ago in North
Beach. She was hustling for a spade pimp. It's
kind of weird. Most women have the temperament
to be a whore, but she's one of these rare
women who just don't have it - the whore
temperament. She's Negro, too.

'She was a teenage girl living on a farm in
Oklahoma. The pimp drove by one afternoon and saw
her playing in the front yard. He stopped his car
and got out and talked to her father for a while.

'I guess he gave her father some money. He
came up with something good because her father
told her to go and get her things. So she went
with the pimp. Simple as that.

'He took her to San Francisco and turned her
out and she hated it. He kept her in line by
terrorizing her all the time. He was a real
sweetheart.

'She had some brains, so he got her a job with

the telephone company during the day, and he
had her hustling at night.

'When Art took her away from him, he got
pretty mad. A good thing and all that. He used
to break into Art's hotel room in the middle of
the night and put a switchblade to Art's throat
and rant and rave. Art kept putting bigger and
bigger locks on the door, but the pimp just kept
breaking in - a huge fellow.

'So Art went out and got a .32 pistol, and the
next time the pimp broke in, Art pulled the
gun out from underneath the covers and jammed it
into the pimp's mouth and said, "You'll be
out of luck the next time you come through that
door, Jack." This broke the pimp up. He never
went back. The pimp certainly lost a good thing.

'He ran up a couple thousand dollars worth of
bills in her name, charge accounts and the like.
They're still paying them off.

'The pistol's right there beside the bed, just
in case the pimp has an attack of amnesia and
wants to have his shoes shined in a funeral
parlour.

'When we go up there, he'll drink the wine.
She won't. She'll have a little bottle of
brandy. She won't offer us any of it. She
drinks about four of them a day. Never buys a
fifth. She always keeps going out and getting
another half-pint.

'That's the way she handles it. She doesn't
talk very much, and she doesn't make any bad
scenes. A good-looking woman.'

My friend knocked on the door and we could hear
somebody get up off the bed and come to the door.

'Who's there?' said a man on the other side.

'Me,' my friend said, in a voice deep and
recognizable as any name.

'I'll open the door.' A simple declarative

91

sentence. He undid about a hundred locks, bolts
and chains and anchors and steel spikes and
canes filled with acid, and then the door
opened like the classroom of a great university
and everything was in its proper place: the gun
beside the bed and a small bottle of brandy
beside an attractive Negro woman.

There were many flowers and plants growing in
the room, some of them were on the dresser,
surrounded by old photographs. All of the
photographs were of white people, including Art
when he was young and handsome and looked just
like the 1930s.

There were pictures of animals cut out of
magazines and tacked to the wall, with crayola
frames drawn around them and crayola picture
wires drawn holding them to the wall. They were
pictures of kittens and puppies. They looked
just fine.

There was a bowl of goldfish next to the bed,
next to the gun. How religious and intimate the
goldfish and the gun looked together.

They had a cat named 208. They covered the
bathroom floor with newspaper and the cat
crapped on the newspaper. My friend said that
208 thought he was the only cat left in the
world, not having seen another cat since he was
a tiny kitten. They never let him out of the
room. He was a red cat and very aggressive. When
you played with that cat, he really bit you.
Stroke 208's fur and he'd try to disembowel
your hand as if it were a belly stuffed full of
extrasoft intestines.

We sat there and drank and talked about books.
Art had owned a lot of books in Los Angeles,
but they were all gone now. He told us that he
used to spend his spare time in secondhand
bookstores buying old and unusual books when he

was in show business, travelling from city to
city across America. Some of them were very rare
autographed books, he told us, but he had bought
them for very little and was forced to sell
them for very little.

'They'd be worth a lot of money now,' he said.

The Negro woman sat there very quietly
studying her brandy. A couple of times she said
yes, in a sort of nice way. She used the word
yes to its best advantage, when surrounded by no
meaning and left alone from other words.

They did their own cooking in the room and had
a single hot plate sitting on the floor, next
to half a dozen plants, including a peach tree
growing in a coffee can. Their closet was
stuffed with food. Along with shirts, suits and
dresses, were canned goods, eggs and cooking oil.

My friend told me that she was a very fine
cook. That she could really cook up a good meal,
fancy dishes, too, on that single hot plate,
next to the peach tree.

They had a good world going for them. He had
such a soft voice and manner that he worked as
a private nurse for rich mental patients. He
made good money when he worked, but sometimes he
was sick himself. He was kind of run down.
She was still working for the telephone company,
but she wasn't doing that night work any more.

They were still paying off the bills that pimp
had run up. I mean, years had passed and they
were still paying them off: a Cadillac and a
hi-fi set and expensive clothes and all those
things that Negro pimps do love to have.

I went back there half-a-dozen times after
that first meeting. An interesting thing
happened. I pretended that the cat, 208, was
named after their room number, though I knew
that their number was in the three hundreds. The

room was on the third floor. It was that simple.

I always went to their room following the geography of Hotel Trout Fishing in America, rather than its numerical layout. I never knew what the exact number of their room was. I knew secretly it was in the three hundreds and that was all.

Anyway, it was easier for me to establish order in my mind by pretending that the cat was named after their room number. It seemed like a good idea and the logical reason for a cat to have the name 208. It, of course, was not true. It was a fib. The cat's name was 208 and the room number was in the three hundreds.

Where did the name 208 come from? What did it mean? I thought about it for a while, hiding it from the rest of my mind. But I didn't ruin my birthday by secretly thinking about it too hard.

A year later I found out the true significance of 208's name, purely by accident. My telephone rang one Saturday morning when the sun was shining on the hills. It was a close friend of mine and he said, 'I'm in the slammer. Come and get me out. They're burning black candles around the drunk tank.'

I went down to the Hall of Justice to bail my friend out, and discovered that 208 is the room number of the bail office. It was very simple. I paid ten dollars for my friend's life and found the original meaning of 208, how it runs like melting snow all the way down the mountainside to a small cat living and playing in Hotel Trout Fishing in America, believing itself to be the last cat in the world, not having seen another cat in such a long time, totally unafraid, newspaper spread out all over the bathroom floor, and something good cooking on the hot plate.

THE SURGEON

I watched my day begin on Little Redfish Lake as
clearly as the first light of dawn or the first
ray of the sunrise, though the dawn and the
sunrise had long since passed and it was now
late in the morning.

The surgeon took a knife from the sheath at
his belt and cut the throat of the chub with a
very gentle motion, showing poetically how sharp
the knife was, and then he heaved the fish back
out into the lake.

The chub made an awkward dead splash and
obeyed all the traffic laws of this world
SCHOOL ZONE SPEED 25 MILES and sank to the cold
bottom of the lake. It lay there white belly up
like a school bus covered with snow. A trout
swam over and took a look, just putting in time,
and swam away.

The surgeon and I were talking about the AMA.
I don't know how in the hell we got on the
thing, but we were on it. Then he wiped the
knife off and put it back in the sheath. I
actually don't know how we got on the AMA.

The surgeon said that he had spent twenty-five
years becoming a doctor. His studies had been
interrupted by the Depression and two wars. He
told me that he would give up the practice of
medicine if it became socialized in America.

'I've never turned away a patient in my life,
and I've never known another doctor who has.
Last year I wrote off six thousand dollars
worth of bad debts,' he said.

I was going to say that a sick person should
never under any conditions be a bad debt, but I
decided to forget it. Nothing was going to be
proved or changed on the shores of Little
Redfish Lake, and as that chub had discovered,
it was not a good place to have cosmetic surgery
done.

'I worked three years ago for a union in
Southern Utah that had a health plan,' the
surgeon said. 'I would not care to practise
medicine under such conditions. The patients
think they own you and your time. They think
you're their own personal garbage can.

'I'd be home eating dinner and the telephone
would ring, "Help! Doctor! I'm dying! It's my
stomach! I've got horrible pains!" I would get
up from my dinner and rush over there.

'The guy would meet me at the door with a can
of beer in his hand. "Hi, doc, come on in. I'll
get you a beer. I'm watching TV. The pain's
all gone. Great, huh? I feel like a million. Sit
down. I'll get you a beer, doc. The Ed
Sullivan Show's on."

'No thank you,' the surgeon said. 'I wouldn't
care to practise medicine under such conditions.
No thank you. No thanks.

'I like to hunt and I like to fish,' he said.
'That's why I moved to Twin Falls. I'd heard so
much about Idaho hunting and fishing. I've been

96

very disappointed. I've given up my practice, sold my home in Twin, and now I'm looking for a new place to settle down.

'I've written to Montana, Wyoming, Colorado, New Mexico, Arizona, California, Nevada, Oregon and Washington for their hunting and fishing regulations, and I've studying them all,' he said.

'I've got enough money to travel around for six months, looking for a place to settle down where the hunting and fishing is good. I'll get twelve hundred dollars back in income tax returns by not working any more this year. That's two hundred a month for not working. I don't understand this country,' he said.

The surgeon's wife and children were in a trailer nearby. The trailer had come in the night before, pulled by a brand-new Rambler station wagon. He had two children, a boy two-and-a-half years old and the other, an infant born prematurely, but now almost up to normal weight.

The surgeon told me that they'd come over from camping on Big Lost River where he had caught a fourteen-inch brook trout. He was young looking, though he did not have much hair on his head.

I talked to the surgeon for a little while longer and said goodbye. We were leaving in the afternoon for Lake Josephus, located at the edge of the Idaho Wilderness, and he was leaving for America, often only a place in the mind.

A NOTE ON THE CAMPING CRAZE THAT IS CURRENTLY SWEEPING AMERICA

As much as anything else, the Coleman lantern is the symbol of the camping craze that is currently sweeping America, with its unholy white light burning in the forests of America.

Last summer, a Mr Norris was drinking at a bar in San Francisco. It was Sunday night and he'd had six or seven. Turning to the guy on the next stool, he said, 'What are you up to?'

'Just having a few,' the guy said.

'That's what I'm doing,' Mr Norris said. 'I like it.'

'I know what you mean,' the guy said. 'I had to lay off for a couple years. I'm just starting up again.'

'What was wrong?' Mr Norris said.

'I had a hole in my liver,' the guy said.

'In your liver?'

'Yeah, the doctor said it was big enough to wave a flag in. It's better now. I can have a couple once in a while. I'm not supposed to, but it won't kill me.'

'Well, I'm thirty-two years old,' Mr Norris

said. 'I've had three wives and I can't
remember the names of my children.'

The guy on the next stool, like a bird on the
next island, took a sip from his Scotch and
soda. The guy liked the sound of the alcohol in
his drink. He put the glass back on the bar.

'That's no problem,' he said to Mr Norris.
'The best thing I know for remembering the
names of children from previous marriages, is to
go out camping, try a little trout fishing.
Trout fishing is one of the best things in the
world for remembering children's names.'

'Is that right?' Mr Norris said.

'Yeah,' the guy said.

'That sounds like an idea,' Mr Norris said.
'I've got to do something. Sometimes I think one
of them is named Carl, but that's impossible.
My third-ex hated the name Carl.'

'You try some camping and that trout fishing,'
the guy on the next stool said. 'And you'll
remember the names of your unborn children.'

'Carl! Carl! Your mother wants you!' Mr Norris
yelled as a kind of joke, then he realized that
it wasn't very funny. He was getting there.

He'd have a couple more and then his head
would always fall forward and hit the bar like a
gunshot. He'd always miss his glass, so he
wouldn't cut his face. His head would always
jump and look startled around the bar, people
staring at it. He'd get up then, and take it
home.

The next morning Mr Norris went down to a
sporting goods store and charged his equipment.
He charged a 9 x 9 foot dry finish tent with an
aluminium centre pole. Then he charged an Arctic
sleeping bag filled with eiderdown and an air
mattress and an air pillow to go with the
sleeping bag. He also charged an air alarm

clock to go along with the idea of night and
waking in the morning.

He charged a two-burner Coleman stove and a
Coleman lantern and a folding aluminium table
and a big set of interlocking aluminium cookware
and a portable ice box.

The last things he charged were his fishing
tackle and a bottle of insect repellent.

He left the next day for the mountains.

Hours later, when he arrived in the mountains,
the first sixteen campgrounds he stopped at
were filled with people. He was a little
surprised. He had no idea the mountains would be
so crowded.

At the seventeenth campground, a man had just
died of a heart attack and the ambulance
attendants were taking down his tent. They
lowered the centre pole and then pulled up the
corner stakes. They folded the tent neatly and
put it in the back of the ambulance, right
beside the man's body.

They drove off down the road, leaving behind
them in the air, a cloud of brilliant white
dust. The dust looked like the light from a
Coleman lantern.

Mr Norris pitched his tent right there and set
up all his equipment and soon had it all going
at once. After he finished eating a dehydrated
beef Stroganoff dinner, he turned off all his
equipment with the master air switch and went to
sleep, for it was now dark.

It was about midnight when they brought the
body and placed it beside the tent, less than a
foot away from where Mr Norris was sleeping in
his Arctic sleeping bag.

He was awakened when they brought the body.
They weren't exactly the quietest body bringers
in the world. Mr Norris could see the bulge of

the body against the side of the tent. The only
thing that separated him from the dead body was
a thin layer of 6 oz water resistant and mildew
resistant DRY FINISH green AMERIFLEX poplin.

Mr Norris un-zipped his sleeping bag and went
outside with a gigantic hound-like flashlight.
He saw the body bringers walking down the path
towards the creek.

'Hey, you guys!' Mr Norris shouted. 'Come back
here. You forgot something.'

'What do you mean?' one of them said. They
both looked very sheepish, caught in the teeth
of the flashlight.

'You know what I mean,' Mr Norris said. 'Right
now!'

The body bringers shrugged their shoulders,
looked at each other and then reluctantly went
back, dragging their feet like children all the
way. They picked up the body. It was heavy and
one of them had trouble getting hold of the
feet.

That one said, kind of hopelessly to Mr
Norris, 'You won't change your mind?'

'Goodnight and goodbye,' Mr Norris said.

They went off down the path towards the creek,
carrying the body between them. Mr Norris turned
his flashlight off and he could hear them,
stumbling over the rocks along the bank of the
creek. He could hear them swearing at each
other. He heard one of them say, 'Hold your
end up.' Then he couldn't hear anything.

About ten minutes later he saw all sorts of
lights go on at another campsite down along the
creek. He heard a distant voice shouting, 'The
answer is no! You already woke up the kids. They
have to have their rest. We're going on a
four-mile hike tomorrow up to Fish Konk Lake.
Try someplace else.'

101

A RETURN TO THE COVER OF THIS BOOK

Dear Trout Fishing in America:

I met your friend Fritz in Washington Square.
He told me to tell you that his case went to
a jury and that he was acquitted by the jury.

He said that it was important for me to say
that his case went to a jury and that he was
acquitted by the jury, so I've said it again.

He looked in good shape. He was sitting in the
sun. There's an old San Francisco saying that
goes: 'It's better to rest in Washington Square
than in the California Adult Authority.'

How are things in New York?

Yours,

'An Ardent Admirer'

Dear Ardent Admirer:

It's good to hear that Fritz isn't in jail.
He was very worried about it. The last time I

was in San Francisco, he told me he thought the
odds were 10-1 in favour of him going away.
I told him to get a good lawyer. It appears that
he followed my advice and also was very lucky.
That's always a good combination.

You asked about New York and New York is very
hot.

I'm visiting some friends, a young burglar and
his wife. He's unemployed and his wife is
working as a cocktail waitress. He's been
looking for work but I fear the worst.

It was so hot last night that I slept with a
wet sheet wrapped around myself, trying to keep
cool. I felt like a mental patient.

I woke up in the middle of the night and the
room was filled with steam rising off the sheet,
and there was jungle stuff, abandoned equipment
and tropical flowers, on the floor and on the
furniture.

I took the sheet into the bathroom and
plopped it into the tub and turned the cold
water on it. Their dog came in and started
barking at me.

The dog barked so loud that the bathroom was
soon filled with dead people. One of them
wanted to use my wet sheet for a shroud. I said
no, and we got into a big argument over it and
woke up the Puerto Ricans in the next apartment,
and they began pounding on the walls.

The dead people all left in a huff. 'We know
when we're not wanted,' one of them said.

'You're damn tootin',' I said.

I've had enough.

I'm going to get out of New York. Tomorrow I'm
leaving for Alaska. I'm going to find an ice-
cold creek near the Arctic where that strange
beautiful moss grows and spend a week with the
grayling. My address will be, Trout Fishing in

America, c/o General Delivery, Fairbanks,
Alaska.

                              Your friend,

                              Trout Fishing in America

THE LAKE JOSEPHUS DAYS

We left Little Redfish for Lake Josephus,
travelling along the good names – from Stanley
to Capehorn to Seafoam to the Rapid River, up
Float Creek, past the Greyhound Mine and then to
Lake Josephus, and a few days after that up the
trail to Hell-diver Lake with the baby on my
shoulders and a good limit of trout waiting in
Hell-diver.

Knowing the trout would wait there like aeroplane tickets for us to come, we stopped at
Mushroom Springs and had a drink of cold
shadowy water and some photographs taken of
the baby and me sitting together on a log.

I hope someday we'll have enough money to get
those pictures developed. Sometimes I get
curious about them, wondering if they will turn
out all right. They are in suspension now like
seeds in a package. I'll be older when they are
developed and easier to please. Look there's the
baby! Look there's Mushroom Springs! Look
there's me!

I caught the limit of trout within an hour of

reaching Hell-diver, and my woman, in all the excitement of good fishing, let the baby fall asleep directly in the sun and when the baby woke up, she puked and I carried her back down the trail.

My woman trailed silently behind, carrying the rods and the fish. The baby puked a couple more times, thimblefuls of gentle lavender vomit, but still it got on my clothes, and her face was hot and flushed.

We stopped at Mushroom Springs. I gave her a small drink of water, not too much, and rinsed the vomit taste out of her mouth. Then I wiped the puke off my clothes and for some strange reason suddenly it was a perfect time, there at Mushroom Springs, to wonder whatever happened to the Zoot suit.

Along with World War II and the Andrews Sisters, the Zoot suit had been very popular in the early 40s. I guess they were all just passing fads.

A sick baby on the trail down from Hell-diver, July 1961, is probably a more important question. It cannot be left to go on forever, a sick baby to take her place in the galaxy, among the comets, bound to pass close to the earth every 173 years.

She stopped puking after Mushroom Springs, and I carried her back down along the path in and out of the shadows and across other nameless springs, and by the time we got down to Lake Josephus, she was all right.

She was soon running around with a big cutthroat trout in her hands, carrying it like a harp on her way to a concert - ten minutes late with no bus in sight and no taxi either.

TROUT FISHING ON THE STREET OF ETERNITY

Calle de Eternidad: We walked up from Gelatao,
birthplace of Benito Juarez. Instead of taking
the road we followed a path up along the creek.
Some boys from the school in Gelatao told us
that up along the creek was the shortcut.

The creek was clear but a little milky, and as
I remember the path was steep in places. We met
people coming down the path because it was
really the shortcut. They were all Indians
carrying something.

Finally the path went away from the creek and
we climbed a hill and arrived at the cemetery.
It was a very old cemetery and kind of run down
with weeds and death growing there like partners
in a dance.

There was a cobblestone street leading up from
the cemetery to the town of Ixtlan, pronounced
East-LON, on top of another hill. There were
no houses along the street until you reached the
town.

In the hair of the world, the street was very
steep as you went up into Ixtlan. There was

a street sign that pointed back down towards the
cemetery, following every cobblestone with
loving care all the way.

We were still out of breath from the climb.
The sign said Calle de Eternidad. Pointing.

I was not always a world traveller, visiting
exotic places in Southern Mexico. Once I was
just a kid working for an old woman in the
Pacific North-west. She was in her nineties and
I worked for her on Saturdays and after school
and during the summer.

Sometimes she would make me lunch, little egg
sandwiches with the crusts cut off as if by a
surgeon, and she'd give me slices of banana
dunked in mayonnaise.

The old woman lived by herself in a house that
was like a twin sister to her. The house was
four storeys high and had at least thirty rooms
and the old lady was five feet high and weighed
about eighty-two pounds.

She had a big radio from the 1920s in the
living-room and it was the only thing in the
house that looked remotely as if it had come
from this century, and then there was still a
doubt in my mind.

A lot of cars, aeroplanes and vacuum cleaners
and refrigerators and things that come from
the 1920s look as if they had come from the
1890s. It's the beauty of our speed that has
done it to them, causing them to age prematurely
into the clothes and thoughts of people from
another century.

The old woman had an old dog, but he hardly
counted any more. He was so old that he looked
like a stuffed dog. Once I took him for a walk
down to the store. It was just like taking a
stuffed dog for a walk. I tied him up to a
stuffed fire hydrant and he pissed on it, but it

was only stuffed piss.

I went into the store and bought some stuffing for the old lady. Maybe a pound of coffee or a quart of mayonnaise.

I did things for her like chop the Canadian thistles. During the 1920s (or was it the 1890s) she was motoring in California, and her husband stopped the car at a filling station and told the attendant to fill it up.

'How about some wild flower seeds?' the attendant said.

'No,' her husband said. 'Gasoline.'

'I know that, sir,' the attendant said. 'But we're giving away wild flower seeds with the gasoline today.'

'All right,' her husband said. 'Give us some wild flower seeds, then. But be sure and fill the car up with gasoline. Gasoline's what I really want.'

'They'll brighten up your garden, sir.'

'The gasoline?'

'No, sir, the flowers.'

They returned to the North-west, planted the seeds and they were Canadian thistles. Every year I chopped them down and they always grew back. I poured chemicals on them and they always grew back.

Curses were music to their roots. A blow on the back of the neck was like a harpsichord to them. Those Canadian thistles were there for keeps. Thank you, California, for your beautiful wild flowers. I chopped them down every year.

I did other things for her like mow the lawn with a grim old lawnmower. When I first went to work for her, she told me to be careful with that lawnmower. Some itinerant had stopped at her place a few weeks before, asked for some

109

work so he could rent a hotel room and get
something to eat, and she'd said, 'You can mow
the lawn.'

'Thanks, ma'am,' he'd said and went out and
promptly cut three fingers off his right hand
with that medieval machine.

I was always very careful with that lawnmower,
knowing that somewhere on that place, the
ghosts of three fingers were living it up in the
grand spook manner. They needed no company
from my fingers. My fingers looked just great,
right there on my hands.

I cleaned out her rock garden and deported
snakes whenever I found them on her place. She
told me to kill them, but I couldn't see any
percentage in wasting a gartersnake. But I had
to get rid of the things because she always
promised me she'd have a heart attack if she
ever stepped on one of them.

So I'd catch them and deport them to a yard
across the street, where nine old ladies
probably had heart attacks and died from
finding those snakes in their toothbrushes.
Fortunately, I was never around when their
bodies were taken away.

I'd clean the blackberry bushes out of the
lilac bushes. Once in a while she'd give me
some lilacs to take home, and they were always
fine-looking lilacs, and I always felt good,
walking down the street, holding the lilacs high
and proud like glasses of that famous children's
drink: the good flower wine.

I'd chop wood for her stove. She cooked on a
woodstove and heated the place during the
winter with a huge wood furnace that she
manned like the captain of a submarine in a dark
basement ocean during the winter.

In the summer I'd throw endless cords of wood

110

into her basement until I was silly in the head
and everything looked like wood, even clouds in
the sky and cars parked on the street and cats.

There were dozens of little tiny things that I
did for her. Find a lost screwdriver, lost in
1911. Pick her a pan full of pie cherries in the
spring, and pick the rest of the cherries on
the tree for myself. Prune those goofy, at
best half-assed trees in the backyard. The ones
that grew beside an old pile of lumber. Weed.

One early autumn day she loaned me to the
woman next door and I fixed a small leak in the
roof on her woodshed. The woman gave me a
dollar tip, and I said thank you, and the next
time it rained, all the newspapers she had been
saving for seventeen years to start fires with
got soaking wet. From then on out, I received a
sour look every time I passed her house. I was
lucky I wasn't lynched.

I didn't work for the old lady in the winter.
I'd finish the year by the last of October,
raking up leaves or something or transporting
the last muttering gartersnake to winter
quarters in the old ladies' toothbrush Valhalla
across the street.

Then she'd call me on the telephone in the
spring. I would always be surprised to hear her
little voice, surprised that she was still
alive. I'd get on my horse and go out to her
place and the whole thing would begin again
and I'd make a few bucks and stroke the
sun-warmed fur of her stuffed dog.

One spring day she had me ascend to the attic
and clean up some boxes of stuff and throw out
some stuff and put some stuff back into its
imaginary proper place.

I was up there all alone for three hours. It
was my first time up there and my last, thank

God. The attic was stuffed to the gills with stuff.

Everything that's old in this world was up there. I spent most of my time just looking around.

An old trunk caught my eye. I unstrapped the straps, unclicked the various clickers and opened the God-damn thing. It was stuffed with old fishing tackle. There were old rods and reels and lines and boots and creels and there was a metal box full of flies and lures and hooks.

Some of the hooks still had worms on them. The worms were years and decades old and petrified to the hooks. The worms were now as much a part of the hooks as the metal itself.

There was some old Trout Fishing in America armour in the trunk and beside a weather-beaten fishing helmet, I saw an old diary. I opened the diary to the first page and it said:

The Trout Fishing Diary of Alonso Hagen

It seemed to me that was the name of the old lady's brother who had died of a strange ailment in his youth, a thing I found out by keeping my ears open and looking at a large photograph prominently displayed in her front room.

I turned to the next page in the old diary and it had in columns:

The Trips and The Trout Lost

April	7, 1891	Trout Lost	8
April	15, 1891	Trout Lost	6
April	23, 1891	Trout Lost	12
May	13, 1891	Trout Lost	9

```
May         23, 1891    Trout Lost  15
May         24, 1891    Trout Lost  10
May         25, 1891    Trout Lost  12
June         2, 1891    Trout Lost  18
June         6, 1891    Trout Lost  15
June        17, 1891    Trout Lost   7
June        19, 1891    Trout Lost  10
June        23, 1891    Trout Lost  14
July         4, 1891    Trout Lost  13
July        23, 1891    Trout Lost  11
August      10, 1891    Trout Lost  13
August      17, 1891    Trout Lost   8
August      20, 1891    Trout Lost  12
August      29, 1891    Trout Lost  21
September    3, 1891    Trout Lost  10
September   11, 1891    Trout Lost   7
September   19, 1891    Trout Lost   5
September   23, 1891    Trout Lost   3
                                   ---
```

Total Trips 22   Total Trout Lost 239
Average Number of Trout Lost Each Trip 10.8

I turned to the third page and it was just like the preceding page except the year was 1892 and Alonso Hagen went on 24 trips and lost 317 trout for an average of 13.2 trout lost each trip.

The next page was 1893 and the totals were 33 trips and 480 trout lost for an average of 14.5 trout lost each trip.

The next page was 1894. He went on 27 trips, lost 349 trout for an average of 12.9 trout lost each trip.

The next page was 1895. He went on 41 trips, lost 730 trout for an average of 17.8 trout lost each trip.

The next page was 1896. Alonso Hagen only went

out 12 times and lost 115 trout for an average
of 9.5 trout lost each trip.

The next page was 1897. He went on one trip
and lost one trout for an average of one trout
lost for one trip.

The last page of the diary was the grand
totals for the years running from 1891-1897.
Alonso Hagen went fishing 160 times and lost
2,231 trout for a seven-year average of 13.9
trout lost every time he went fishing.

Under the grand totals, there was a little
Trout Fishing in America epitaph by Alonso
Hagen. It said something like:

'I've had it.

I've gone fishing now for seven years

and I haven't caught a single trout.

I've lost every trout I ever hooked.

They either jump off

or twist off.

or squirm off

or break my leader

or flop off

or fuck off.

I have never even gotten my hands on a trout.

For all its frustration,

I believe it was an interesting experiment

in total loss

but next year somebody else

will have to go trout fishing.

Somebody else will have to go

out there.'

114

THE TOWEL

We came down the road from Lake Josephus and
down the road from Seafoam. We stopped along
the way to get a drink of water. There was a
small monument in the forest. I walked over to
the monument to see what was happening. The
glass door of the lookout was partly open and
a towel was hanging on the other side.

At the centre of the monument was a
photograph. It was the classic forest lookout
photograph I have seen before, from that
America that existed during the 1920s and 30s.

There was a man in the photograph who looked a
lot like Charles A. Lindbergh. He had that same
Spirit of St Louis nobility and purpose of
expression, except that his North Atlantic was
the forests of Idaho.

There was a woman cuddled up close to him. She
was one of those great cuddly women of the
past, wearing those pants they used to wear and
those hightop, laced boots.

They were standing on the porch of the
lookout. The sky was behind them, no more than a

few feet away. People in those days liked to
take that photograph and they liked to be in it.
There were words on the monument. They said:

     'In memory of Charley J. Langer, District
    Forest Ranger, Challis National Forest,
    Pilot Captain Bill Kelly and Co-Pilot
    Arthur A. Crofts, of the U.S. Army
    killed in an Airplane Crash April 5, 1943,
    near this point while searching for
    survivors of an Army Bomber Crew.'

O it's far away now in the mountains that a
photograph guards the memory of a man. The
photograph is all alone out there. The snow is
falling eighteen years after his death. It
covers up the door. It covers up the towel.

SANDBOX MINUS JOHN DILLINGER EQUALS WHAT?

Often I return to the cover of Trout Fishing in
America. I took the baby and went down there
this morning. They were watering the cover with
big revolving sprinklers. I saw some bread
lying on the grass. It had been put there to
feed the pigeons.

The old Italians are always doing things like
that. The bread had been turned to paste by the
water and was squashed flat against the grass.
Those dopey pigeons were waiting until the water
and grass had chewed up the bread for them, so
they wouldn't have to do it themselves.

I let the baby play in the sandbox and I sat
down on a bench and looked around. There was a
beatnik sitting at the other end of the bench.
He had his sleeping bag beside him and he was
eating apple turnovers. He had a huge sack of
apple turnovers and he was gobbling them down
like a turkey. It was probably a more valid
protest than picketing missile bases.

The baby played in the sandbox. She had on a
red dress and the Catholic church was towering

up behind her red dress. There was a brick john
between her dress and the church. It was there
by no accident. Ladies to the left and gents to
the right.

A red dress, I thought. Wasn't the woman who
set John Dillinger up for the FBI wearing a
red dress? They called her 'The Woman in Red'.

It seemed to me that was right. It was a red
dress, but so far, John Dillinger was nowhere in
sight. My daughter played alone in the sandbox.

Sandbox minus John Dillinger equals what?

The beatnik went and got a drink of water from
the fountain that was crucified on the wall of
the brick john, more towards the gents than
the ladies. He had to wash all those apple
turnovers down his throat.

There were three sprinklers going in the park.
There was one in front of the Benjamin Franklin
statue and one to the side of him and one just
behind him. They were all turning in circles.
I saw Benjamin Franklin standing there patiently
through the water.

The sprinkler to the side of Benjamin Franklin
hit the left-hand tree. It sprayed hard against
the trunk and knocked some leaves down from
the tree, and then it hit the centre tree,
sprayed hard against the trunk and more leaves
fell. Then it sprayed against Benjamin Franklin,
the water shot out to the sides of the stone
and a mist drifted down off the water. Benjamin
Franklin got his feet wet.

The sun was shining down hard on me. The sun
was bright and hot. After a while the sun made
me think of my own discomfort. The only shade
fell on the beatnik.

The shade came down off the Little Hitchcock
Coit statue of some metal fireman saving a
metal broad from a mental fire. The beatnik now

118

lay on the bench and the shade was two feet longer than he was.

A friend of mine has written a poem about that statue. God-damn, I wish he would write another poem about that statue, so it would give me some shade two feet longer than my body.

I was right about 'The Woman in Red', because ten minutes later they blasted John Dillinger down in the sandbox. The sound of the machine-gun fire startled the pigeons and they hurried on into the church.

My daughter was seen leaving in a huge black car shortly after that. She couldn't talk yet, but that didn't make any difference. The red dress did it all.

John Dillinger's body lay half in and half out of the sandbox, more towards the ladies than the gents. He was leaking blood like those capsules we used to use with oleomargarine, in those good old days when oleo was white like lard.

The huge black car pulled out and went up the street, bat-light shining off the top. It stopped in front of the ice-cream parlour at Filbert and Stockton.

An agent got out and went in and bought two hundred double-decker ice-cream cones. He needed a wheelbarrow to get them back to the car.

THE LAST TIME I SAW TROUT FISHING IN AMERICA

The last time we met was in July on the Big Wood
River, ten miles away from Ketchum. It was just
after Hemingway had killed himself there, but
I didn't know about his death at the time. I
didn't know about it until I got back to San
Francisco weeks after the thing had happened and
picked up a copy of Life magazine. There was a
photograph of Hemingway on the cover.

'I wonder what Hemingway's up to,' I said to
myself. I looked inside the magazine and turned
the pages to his death. Trout Fishing in
America forgot to tell me about it. I'm certain
he knew. It must have slipped his mind.

The woman who travels with me had menstrual
cramps. She wanted to rest for a while, so I
took the baby and my spinning rod and went
down to the Big Wood River. That's where I met
Trout Fishing in America.

I was casting a Super-Duper out into the river
and letting it swing down with the current and
then ride on the water up close to the shore.
It fluttered there slowly and Trout Fishing

in America watched the baby while we talked.

I remember that he gave her some coloured rocks to play with. She liked him and climbed up on to his lap and she started putting the rocks in his shirt pocket.

We talked about Great Falls, Montana. I told Trout Fishing in America about a winter I spent as a child in Great Falls. 'It was during the war and I saw a Deanna Durbin movie seven times,' I said.

The baby put a blue rock in Trout Fishing in America's shirt pocket and he said, 'I've been to Great Falls many times. I remember Indians and fur traders. I remember Lewis and Clark, but I don't remember ever seeing a Deanna Durbin movie in Great Falls.'

'I know what you mean,' I said. 'The other people in Great Falls did not share my enthusiasm for Deanna Durbin. The theatre was always empty. There was a darkness to that theatre different from any theatre I've been in since. Maybe it was the snow outside and Deanna Durbin inside. I don't know what it was.'

'What was the name of the movie?' Trout Fishing in America said.

'I don't know,' I said. 'She sang a lot. Maybe she was a chorus girl who wanted to go to college or she was a rich girl or they needed money for something or she did something. Whatever it was about, she sang! and sang! but I can't remember a God-damn word of it.

'One afternoon after I had seen the Deanna Durbin movie again, I went down to the Missouri River. Part of the Missouri was frozen over. There was a railroad bridge there. I was very relieved to see that the Missouri River had not changed and begun to look like Deanna Durbin.

'I'd had a childhood fancy that I would walk

121

down to the Missouri River and it would look
just like a Deanna Durbin movie - a chorus girl
who wanted to go to college or she was a rich
girl or they needed money for something or she
did something.

'To this day I don't know why I saw that
movie seven times. It was just as deadly as
The Cabinet of Doctor Caligari. I wonder if
the Missouri River is still there?' I said.

'It is,' Trout Fishing in America said smiling.
'But it doesn't look like Deanna Durbin.'

The baby by this time had put a dozen or so of
the coloured rocks in Trout Fishing in America's
shirt pocket. He looked at me and smiled and
waited for me to go on about Great Falls, but
just then I had a fair strike on my Super-Duper.
I jerked the rod back and missed the fish.

Trout Fishing in America said, 'I know that
fish who just struck. You'll never catch him.'

'Oh,' I said.

'Forgive me,' Trout Fishing in America said.
'Go on ahead and try for him. He'll hit a
couple of times more, but you won't catch him.
He's not a particularly smart fish. Just lucky.
Sometimes that's all you need.'

'Yeah,' I said. 'You're right there.'

I cast out again and continued talking about
Great Falls.

Then in correct order I recited the twelve
least important things ever said about Great
Falls, Montana. For the twelfth and least
important thing of all, I said, 'Yeah, the
telephone would ring in the morning. I'd get out
of bed. I didn't have to answer the telephone. That
had all been taken care of, years in advance.

'It would still be dark outside and the yellow
wallpaper in the hotel room would be running
back off the light bulb. I'd put my clothes on

122

and go down to the restaurant where my step-father cooked all night.

'I'd have breakfast, hot cakes, eggs and whatnot. Then he'd make my lunch for me and it would always be the same thing: a piece of pie and a stone-cold pork sandwich. Afterwards I'd walk to school. I mean the three of us, the Holy Trinity: me, a piece of pie, and a stone-cold pork sandwich. This went on for months.

'Fortunately it stopped one day without my having to do anything serious like grow up. We packed our stuff and left town on a bus. That was Great Falls, Montana. You say the Missouri River is still there?'

'Yes, but it doesn't look like Deanna Durbin,' Trout Fishing in America said. 'I remember the day Lewis discovered the falls. They left their camp at sunrise and a few hours later they came upon a beautiful plain and on the plain were more buffalo than they had ever seen before in one place.

'They kept on going until they heard the faraway sound of a waterfall and saw a distant column of spray rising and disappearing. They followed the sound as it got louder and louder. After a while the sound was tremendous and they were at the great falls of the Missouri River. It was about noon when they got there.

'A nice thing happened that afternoon, they went fishing below the falls and caught half a dozen trout, good ones, too, from sixteen to twenty-three inches long.

'That was June 13, 1805.

'No, I don't think Lewis would have understood it if the Missouri River had suddenly begun to look like a Deanna Durbin movie, like a chorus girl who wanted to go to college,' Trout Fishing in America said.

IN THE CALIFORNIA BUSH

I've come home from Trout Fishing in America,
the highway bent its long smooth anchor about my
neck and then stopped. Now I live in this place.
It took my whole life to get here, to get to
this strange cabin above Mill Valley.

We're staying with Pard and his girlfriend.
They have rented a cabin for three months,
June 15 to September 15, for a hundred dollars.
We are a funny bunch, all living here together.

Pard was born of Okie parents in British
Nigeria and came to America when he was two
years old and was raised as a ranch kid in
Oregon, Washington and Idaho.

He was a machine-gunner in the Second World
War, against the Germans. He fought in France
and Germany. Sergeant Pard. Then he came back
from the war and went to some hick college in
Idaho.

After he graduated from college, he went to
Paris and became an Existentialist. He had a
photograph taken of Existentialism and himself
sitting at a sidewalk cafe. Pard was wearing a

beard and he looked as if he had a huge soul,
with barely enough room in his body to contain it.

When Pard came back to America from Paris, he
worked as a tugboat man on San Francisco Bay and
as a railroad man in the roundhouse at Filer,
Idaho.

Of course, during this time he got married and
had a kid. The wife and kid are gone now,
blown away like apples by the fickle wind of the
Twentieth Century. I guess the fickle wind of
all time. The family that fell in the autumn.

After he split up with his wife, he went to
Arizona and was a reporter and editor of
newspapers. He honky-tonked in Naco, a Mexican
border town, drank Mescal Triunfo, played cards
and shot the roof of his house full of bullet
holes.

Pard tells a story about waking one morning in
Naco, all hungover, with the whips and jingles.
A friend of his was sitting at the table with a
bottle of whisky beside him.

Pard reached over and picked up a gun off a
chair and took aim at the whisky bottle and
fired. His friend was then sitting there,
covered with flecks of glass, blood and whisky.
'What the fuck you do that for?' he said.

Now in his late thirties Pard works at a print
shop for $1.35 an hour. It is an avant-garde
print shop. They print poetry and experimental
prose. They pay him $1.35 an hour for operating
a linotype machine. A $1.35 linotype operator is
hard to find, outside of Hong Kong or Albania.

Sometimes when he goes down there, they don't
even have enough lead for him. They buy their
lead like soap, a bar or two at a time.

Pard's girlfriend is a Jew. Twenty-four years
old, getting over a bad case of hepatitis, she
kids Pard about a nude photograph of her that

has the possibility of appearing in Playboy
magazine.

'There's nothing to worry about,' she says.
'If they use that photograph, it only means that
12,000,000 men will look at my boobs.'

This is all very funny to her. Her parents
have money. As she sits in the other room in the
California bush, she's on her father's payroll
in New York.

What we eat is funny and what we drink is even
more hilarious: turkeys, Gallo port, hot dogs,
watermelons, Popeyes, salmon croquettes,
frappes, Christian Brothers port, orange rye
bread, canteloupes, Popeyes, salads, cheese –
booze, grub and Popeyes.

Popeyes?

We read books like The Thief's Journal,
Set This House on Fire, The Naked Lunch,
Krafft-Ebing. We read Krafft-Ebing aloud all
the time as if he were Kraft dinner.

'The mayor of a small town in Eastern Portugal
was seen one morning pushing a wheelbarrow full
of sex organs into the city hall. He was of
tainted family. He had a woman's shoe in his
back pocket. It had been there all night.'
Things like this make us laugh.

The woman who owns this cabin will come back
in the autumn. She's spending the summer in
Europe. When she comes back, she will spend only
one day a week out here: Saturday. She will
never spend the night because she's afraid to.
There is something here that makes her afraid.

Pard and his girlfriend sleep in the cabin and
the baby sleeps in the basement, and we sleep
outside, under the apple tree, waking at dawn
to stare out across San Francisco Bay and then
we go back to sleep again and wake once more,

this time for a very strange thing to happen, and then we go back to sleep again after it has happened, and wake at sunrise to stare out across the bay.

Afterwards we go back to sleep again and the sun rises steadily hour after hour, staying in the branches of a eucalyptus tree just a ways down the hill, keeping us cool and asleep and in the shade. At last the sun pours over the top of the tree and then we have to get up, the hot sun upon us.

We go into the house and begin that two-hour yak-yak activity we call breakfast. We sit around and bring ourselves slowly back to consciousness, treating ourselves like fine pieces of china, and after we finish the last cup of the last cup of the last cup of coffee, it's time to think about lunch or go to the Goodwill in Fairfax.

So here we are, living in the California bush above Mill Valley. We could look right down on the main street of Mill Valley if it were not for the eucalyptus tree. We have to park the car a hundred yards away and come here along a tunnel-like path.

If all the Germans Pard killed during the war with his machine gun were to come and stand in their uniforms around this place, it would make us pretty nervous.

There's the warm sweet smell of blackberry bushes along the path and in the late afternoon, quail gather around a dead unrequited tree that has fallen bridelike across the path. Sometimes I go down there and jump the quail. I just go down there to get them up off their butts. They're such beautiful birds. They set their wings and sail on down the hill.

O he was the one who was born to be king! That

one, turning down through the Scotch broom and going over an upsidedown car abandoned in the yellow grass. That one, his grey wings.

One morning last week, part way through the dawn, I awoke under the apple tree, to hear a dog barking and the rapid sound of hoofs coming towards me. The millennium? An invasion of Russians all wearing deer feet?

I opened my eyes and saw a deer running straight at me. It was a buck with large horns. There was a police dog chasing after it.

Arfwowfuck! Noisepoundpoundpoundpoundpound! POUND! POUND!

The deer didn't swerve away. He just kept running straight at me, long after he had seen me, a second or two had passed.

Arfwowfuck! Noisepoundpoundpoundpoundpound! POUND! POUND!

I could have reached out and touched him when he went by.

He ran around the house, circling the john, with the dog hot after him. They vanished over the hillside, leaving streamers of toilet paper behind them, flowing out and entangled through the bushes and vines.

Then along came the doe. She started up the same way, but not moving as fast. Maybe she had strawberries in her head.

'Whoa!' I shouted. 'Enough is enough! I'm not selling newspapers!'

The doe stopped in her tracks, twenty-five feet away and turned and went down around the eucalyptus tree.

Well, that's how it's gone now for days and days. I wake up just before they come. I wake up for them in the same manner as I do for the dawn and the sunrise. Suddenly knowing they're on their way.

THE LAST MENTION OF TROUT FISHING IN AMERICA SHORTY

Saturday was the first day of autumn and there was a festival being held at the church of Saint Francis. It was a hot day and the Ferris wheel was turning in the air like a thermometer bent in a circle and given the grace of music.

But all this goes back to another time, to when my daughter was conceived. We'd just moved into a new apartment and the lights hadn't been turned on yet. We were surrounded by unpacked boxes of stuff and there was a candle burning like milk on a saucer. So we got one in and we're sure it was the right one.

A friend was sleeping in another room. In retrospect I hope we didn't wake him up, though he has been awakened and gone to sleep hundreds of times since then.

During the pregnancy I stared innocently at that growing human centre and had no idea the child therein contained would ever meet Trout Fishing in America Shorty.

Saturday afternoon we went down to Washington Square. We put the baby down on the grass and

she took off running towards Trout Fishing in
America Shorty who was sitting under the trees
by the Benjamin Franklin statue.

He was on the ground leaning up against the
right-hand tree. There were some garlic sausages
and some bread sitting in his wheelchair as if
it were a display counter in a strange grocery
store.

The baby ran down there and tried to make off
with one of his sausages.

Trout Fishing in America Shorty was instantly
alerted, then he saw it was a baby and relaxed.
He tried to coax her to come over and sit on his
legless lap. She hid behind his wheelchair,
staring past the metal at him, one of her hands
holding on to a wheel.

'Come here, kid,' he said. 'Come over and see
old Trout Fishing in America Shorty.'

Just then the Benjamin Franklin statue turned
green like a traffic light, and the baby noticed
the sandbox at the other end of the park.

The sandbox suddenly looked better to her than
Trout Fishing in America Shorty. She didn't
care about his sausages any more either.

She decided to take advantage of the green
light, and she crossed over to the sandbox.

Trout Fishing in America Shorty stared after
her as if the space between them were a river
growing larger and larger.

WITNESS FOR TROUT FISHING IN AMERICA PEACE

In San Francisco around Easter time last year,
they had a trout fishing in America peace
parade. They had thousands of red stickers
printed and they pasted them on their small
foreign cars, and on means of national
communication like telephone poles.

The stickers had WITNESS FOR TROUT FISHING
IN AMERICA PEACE printed on them.

Then this group of college- and high-school-
trained Communists, along with some Communist
clergymen and their Marxist-taught children,
marched to San Francisco from Sunnyvale, a
Communist nerve centre about forty miles
away.

It took them four days to walk to San
Francisco. They stopped overnight at various
towns along the way, and slept on the lawns of
fellow travellers.

They carried with them Communist trout fishing
in America peace propaganda posters:

'DON'T DROP AN H-BOMB ON THE OLD FISHING HOLE!'

'ISAAC WALTON WOULD'VE HATED THE BOMB!'

'ROYAL COACHMAN, SI! ICBM, NO!'

They carried with them many other trout fishing in America peace inducements, all following the Communist world conquest line: the Gandhian nonviolence Trojan horse.

When these young, hard-core brainwashed members of the Communist conspiracy reached the 'Panhandle,' the emigre Oklahoma Communist sector of San Francisco, thousands of other Communists were waiting for them. These were Communists who couldn't walk very far. They barely had enough strength to make it downtown.

Thousands of Communists, protected by the police, marched down to Union Square, located in the very heart of San Francisco. The Communist City Hall riots in 1960 had presented evidence of it, the police let hundreds of Communists escape, but the trout fishing in America peace parade was the final indictment: police protection.

Thousands of Communists marched right into the heart of San Francisco, and Communist speakers incited them for hours and the young people wanted to blow up Coit Tower, but the Communist clergy told them to put away their plastic bombs.

'Therefore all things whatsoever ye would that men should do to you, do ye even so to them ... There will be no need for explosives,' they said.

America needs no other proof. The Red shadow of the Gandhian nonviolence Trojan horse has fallen across America, and San Francisco is its stable.

Obsolete is the mad rapist's legendary piece
of candy. At this very moment, Communist agents
are handing out Witness for trout fishing in
America peace tracts to innocent children riding
the cable cars.

FOOTNOTE CHAPTER TO 'RED LIP'

Living in the California bush we had no garbage
service. Our garbage was never greeted in the
early morning by a man with a big smile on his
face and a kind word or two. We couldn't burn
any of the garbage because it was the dry season
and everything was ready to catch on fire
anyway, including ourselves. The garbage was a
problem for a little while and then we
discovered a way to get rid of it.

We took the garbage down to where there were
three abandoned houses in a row. We carried
sacks full of tin cans, papers, peelings,
bottles and Popeyes.

We stopped at the last abandoned house where
there were thousands of old receipts to the San
Francisco Chronicle thrown all over the bed and
the children's toothbrushes were still in the
bathroom medicine cabinet.

Behind the place was an old outhouse and to
get down to it, you had to follow the path down
past some apple trees and a patch of strange
plants that we thought were either a good spice

that would certainly enhance our cooking or the plants were deadly nightshade that would cause our cooking to be less.

We carried the garbage down to the outhouse and always opened the door slowly because that was the only way you could open it, and on the wall there was a roll of toilet paper, so old it looked like a relative, perhaps a cousin, to the Magna Carta.

We lifted up the lid of the toilet and dropped the garbage down into the darkness. This went on for weeks and weeks until it became very funny to lift the lid of the toilet and instead of seeing darkness below or maybe the murky abstract outline of garbage, we saw bright, definite and lusty garbage heaped up almost to the top.

If you were a stranger and went down there to take an innocent crap, you would've had quite a surprise when you lifted up the lid.

We left the California bush just before it became necessary to stand on the toilet seat and step into that hole, crushing the garbage down like an accordion into the abyss.

THE CLEVELAND WRECKING YARD

Until recently my knowledge about the Cleveland
Wrecking Yard had come from a couple of friends
who'd bought things there. One of them bought a
huge window: the frame, glass and everything
for just a few dollars. It was a fine-looking
window.

Then he chopped a hole in the side of his
house up on Potrero Hill and put the window in.
Now he has a panoramic view of the San Francisco
County Hospital.

He can practically look right down into the
wards and see old magazines eroded like the
Grand Canyon from endless readings. He can
practically hear the patients thinking about
breakfast: I hate milk, and thinking about
dinner: I hate peas, and then he can watch the
hospital slowly drown at night, hopelessly
entangled in huge bunches of brick seaweed.

He bought that window at the Cleveland
Wrecking Yard.

My other friend bought an iron roof at the
Cleveland Wrecking Yard and took the roof down

to Big Sur in an old station wagon and then he
carried the iron roof on his back up the side of
a mountain. He carried up half the roof on his
back. It was no picnic. Then he bought a mule,
George, from Pleasanton. George carried up the
other half of the roof.

The mule didn't like what was happening at
all. He lost a lot of weight because of the
ticks, and the smell of the wildcats up on the
plateau made him too nervous to graze there.
My friend said jokingly that George had lost
around two hundred pounds. The good wine country
around Pleasanton in the Livermore Valley
probably had looked a lot better to George than
the wild side of the Santa Lucia Mountains.

My friend's place was a shack right beside a
huge fireplace where there had once been a great
mansion during the 1920s, built by a famous
movie actor. The mansion was built before there
was even a road down at Big Sur. The mansion
had been brought over the mountains on the
backs of mules, strung out like ants, bringing
visions of the good life to the poison oak, the
ticks, and the salmon.

The mansion was on a promontory, high over the
Pacific. Money could see farther in the 1920s,
and one could look out and see whales and the
Hawaiian Islands and the Kuomintang in China.

The mansion burned down years ago.

The actor died.

His mules were made into soap.

His mistresses became bird nests of wrinkles.

Now only the fireplace remains as a sort of
Carthaginian homage to Hollywood.

I was down there a few weeks ago to see my
friend's roof. I wouldn't have passed up the
chance for a million dollars, as they say. The
roof looked like a colander to me. If that roof

and the rain were running against each other at
Bay Meadows, I'd bet on the rain and plan to
spend my winnings at the World's Fair in
Seattle.

My own experience with the Cleveland Wrecking
Yard began two days ago when I heard about a
used trout stream they had on sale out at the
Yard. So I caught the Number 15 bus on Columbus
Avenue and went out there for the first time.

There were two Negro boys sitting behind me on
the bus. They were talking about Chubby Checker
and the Twist. They thought that Chubby Checker
was only fifteen years old because he didn't
have a moustache. Then they talked about some
other guy who did the twist forty-four hours in
a row until he saw George Washington crossing
the Delaware.

'Man, that's what I call twisting,' one of the
kids said.

'I don't think I could twist no forty-four
hours in a row,' the other kid said. 'That's a
lot of twisting.'

I got off the bus right next to an abandoned
Time Gasoline filling station and an
abandoned fifty-cent self-service car wash.
There was a long field on one side of the
filling station. The field had once been covered
with a housing project during the war, put
there for the shipyard workers.

On the other side of the Time filling station
was the Cleveland Wrecking Yard. I walked down
there to have a look at the used trout stream.
The Cleveland Wrecking Yard has a very long
front window filled with signs and merchandise.

There was a sign in the window advertising a
laundry marking machine for $65.00 The original
cost of the machine was $175.00. Quite a saving.

There was another sign advertising new and

138

used two and three ton hoists. I wondered how
many hoists it would take to move a trout
stream.
There was another sign that said:

THE FAMILY GIFT CENTER,
GIFT SUGGESTIONS FOR THE ENTIRE FAMILY

The window was filled with hundreds of items
for the entire family. Daddy, do you know what I
want for Christmas? What, son? A bathroom.
Mommy, do you know what I want for Christmas?
What, Patricia? Some roofing material.
There were jungle hammocks in the window for
distant relatives and dollar-ten-cent gallons
of earth-brown enamel paint for other loved
ones.
There was also a big sign that said:

USED TROUT STREAM FOR SALE.
MUST BE SEEN TO BE APPRECIATED.

I went inside and looked at some ship's lanterns
that were for sale next to the door. Then a
salesman came up to me and said in a pleasant
voice, 'Can I help you?'
'Yes,' I said. 'I'm curious about the trout
stream you have for sale. Can you tell me
something about it? How are you selling it?'
'We're selling it by the foot length. You can
buy as little as you want or you can buy all
we've got left. A man came in here this morning
and bought 563 feet. He's going to give it to
his niece for a birthday present,' the salesman
said.
'We're selling the waterfalls separately of
course, and the trees and birds, flowers, grass

and ferns we're also selling extra. The insects
we're giving away free with a minimum purchase
of ten feet of stream.'

'How much are you selling the stream for?' I
asked.

'Six dollars and fifty-cents a foot,' he said.
'That's for the first hundred feet. After that
it's five dollars a foot.'

'How much are the birds?' I asked.

'Thirty-five cents apiece,' he said. 'But of
course they're used. We can't guarantee
anything.'

'How wide is the stream?' I asked. 'You said
you were selling it by the length, didn't you?'

'Yes,' he said. 'We're selling it by the
length. Its width runs between five and eleven
feet. You don't have to pay anything extra for
width. It's not a big stream, but it's very
pleasant.'

'What kinds of animals do you have?' I asked.

'We only have three deer left,' he said.

'Oh ... What about flowers?'

'By the dozen,' he said.

'Is the stream clear?' I asked.

'Sir,' the salesman said. 'I wouldn't want you
to think that we would ever sell a murky trout
stream here. We always make sure they're
running crystal clear before we even think about
moving them.'

'Where did the stream come from?' I asked.

'Colorado,' he said. 'We moved it with loving
care. We've never damaged a trout stream yet.
We treat them all as if they were china.'

'You're probably asked this all the time, but
how's fishing in the stream?' I asked.

'Very good,' he said. 'Mostly German browns,
but there are a few rainbows.'

'What do the trout cost?' I asked.

'They come with the stream,' he said. 'Of course it's all luck. You never know how many you're going to get or how big they are. But the fishing's very good, you might say it's excellent. Both bait and dry fly,' he said smiling.

'Where's the stream at?' I asked. 'I'd like to take a look at it.'

'It's around in back' he said. 'You go straight through that door and then turn right until you're outside. It's stacked in lengths. You can't miss it. The waterfalls are upstairs in the used plumbing department.'

'What about the animals?'

'Well, what's left of the animals are straight back from the stream. You'll see a bunch of our trucks parked on a road by the railroad tracks. Turn right on the road and follow it down past the piles of lumber. The animal shed's right at the end of the lot.'

'Thanks,' I said. 'I think I'll look at the waterfalls first. You don't have to come with me. Just tell me how to get there and I'll find my own way.'

'All right,' he said. 'Go up those stairs. You'll see a bunch of doors and windows, turn left and you'll find the used plumbing department. Here's my card if you need any help.'

'Okay,' I said. 'You've been a great help already. Thanks a lot. I'll take a look around.'

'Good luck,' he said.

I went upstairs and there were thousands of doors there. I'd never seen so many doors before in my life. You could have built an entire city out of those doors. Doorstown. And there were enough windows up there to build a little suburb entirely out of windows. Windowville.

141

I turned left and went back and saw the faint
glow of pearl-coloured light. The light got
stronger as I went farther back, and then I was
in the used plumbing department, surrounded by
hundreds of toilets.

The toilets were stacked on shelves. They were
stacked five toilets high. There was a skylight
above the toilets that made them glow like the
Great Taboo Pearl of the South Sea movies.

Stacked over against the wall were the waterfalls. There were about a dozen of them,
ranging from a drop of a few feet to a drop of
ten or fifteen feet.

There was one waterfall that was over sixty
feet long. There were tags on the pieces of the
big falls describing the correct order for
putting the falls back together again.

The waterfalls all had price tags on them.
They were more expensive than the stream. The
waterfalls were selling for $19.00 a foot.

I went into another room where there were
piles of sweet-smelling lumber, glowing a soft
yellow from a different colour skylight above
the lumber. In the shadows at the edge of the
room under the sloping roof of the building
were many sinks and urinals covered with dust,
and there was also another waterfall about
seventeen feet long, lying there in two lengths
and already beginning to gather dust.

I had seen all I wanted of the waterfalls, and
now I was very curious about the trout stream,
so I followed the salesman's directions and
ended up outside the building.

O I had never in my life seen anything like
that trout stream. It was stacked in piles of
various lengths: ten, fifteen, twenty feet, etc.
There was one pile of hundred-foot lengths.
There was also a box of scraps. The scraps were

in odd sizes ranging from six inches to a couple
of feet.

There was a loudspeaker on the side of the
building and soft music was coming out. It was a
cloudy day and seagulls were circling high
overhead.

Behind the stream were big bundles of trees
and bushes. They were covered with sheets of
patched canvas. You could see the tops and roots
sticking out the ends of the bundles.

I went up close and looked at the lengths of
stream. I could see some trout in them. I saw
one good fish. I saw some crawdads crawling
around the rocks at the bottom.

It looked like a fine stream. I put my hand in
the water. It was cold and felt good.

I decided to go around to the side and look at
the animals. I saw where the trucks were
parked beside the railroad tracks. I followed
the road down past the piles of lumber, back
to the shed where the animals were.

The salesman had been right. They were
practically out of animals. About the only thing
they had left in any abundance were mice.
There were hundreds of mice.

Beside the shed was a huge wire birdcage,
maybe fifty feet high, filled with many kinds
of birds. The top of the cage had a piece of
canvas over it, so the birds wouldn't get wet
when it rained. There were woodpeckers and wild
canaries and sparrows.

On my way back to where the trout stream was
piled, I found the insects. They were inside a
prefabricated steel building that was selling
for eighty-cents a square foot. There was a
sign over the door. It said

INSECTS

A HALF-SUNDAY HOMAGE TO A WHOLE
LEONARDO DA VINCI

On this funky winter day in rainy San Francisco
I've had a vision of Leonardo da Vinci. My
woman's out slaving away, no day off, working
on Sunday. She left here at eight o'clock this
morning for Powell and California. I've been
sitting here ever since like a toad on a log
dreaming about Leonardo da Vinci.

I dreamt he was on the South Bend Tackle
Company payroll, but of course, he was wearing
different clothes and speaking with a different
accent and possessor of a different childhood,
perhaps an American childhood spent in a town
like Lordsburg, New Mexico, or Winchester,
Virginia.

I saw him inventing a new spinning lure for
trout fishing in America. I saw him first of all
working with his imagination, then with metal
and colour and hooks, trying a little of this
and a little of that, and then adding motion
and then taking it away and then coming back
again with a different motion, and in the end
the lure was invented.

He called his bosses in. They looked at the
lure and all fainted. Alone, standing over their
bodies, he held the lure in his hand and gave it
a name. He called it 'The Last Supper'. Then
he went about waking up his bosses.

In a matter of months that trout fishing lure
was the sensation of the twentieth century, far
outstripping such shallow accomplishments as
Hiroshima or Mahatma Gandhi. Millions of 'The
Last Supper' were sold in America. The Vatican
ordered ten thousand and they didn't even have
any trout there.

Testimonials poured in. Thirty-four ex-
presidents of the United States all said, 'I
caught my limit on "The Last Supper".'

TROUT FISHING IN AMERICA NIB

He went up to Chemault, that's in Eastern
Oregon, to cut Christmas trees. He was working
for a very small enterprise. He cut the trees,
did the cooking and slept on the kitchen floor.
It was cold and there was snow on the ground.
The floor was hard. Somewhere along the line, he
found an old Air Force flight jacket. That
was a big help in the cold.

The only woman he could find up there was a
three-hundred-pound Indian squaw. She had twin
fifteen-year-old daughters and he wanted to
get into them. But the squaw worked it so he
only got into her. She was clever that way.

The people he was working for wouldn't pay him
up there. They said he'd get it all in one sum
when they got back to San Francisco. He'd taken
the job because he was broke, really broke.

He waited and cut trees in the snow, laid the
squaw, cooked bad food - they were on a tight
budget - and he washed the dishes. Afterwards,
he slept on the kitchen floor in his Air Force
flight jacket.

When they finally got back to town with the
trees, those guys didn't have any money to
pay him off. He had to wait around the lot in
Oakland until they sold enough trees to pay
him off.

'Here's a lovely tree, ma'am.'

'How much?'

'Ten dollars.'

'That's too much.'

'I have a lovely two-dollar tree here, ma'am.
Actually, it's only half a tree, but you can
stand it up right next to a wall and it'll look
great, ma'am.'

'I'll take it. I can put it right next to my
weather clock. This tree is the same colour as
the queen's dress. I'll take it. You said two
dollars?'

'That's right, ma'am.'

'Hello, sir. Yes ... Uh-huh ... Yes ... You
say that you want to bury your aunt with a
Christmas tree in her coffin? Uh-huh ... She
wanted it that way ... I'll see what I can do
for you, sir. Oh, you have the measurements of
the coffin with you? Very good ... We have our
coffin-sized Christmas trees right over here,
sir.'

Finally he was paid off and he came over to
San Francisco and had a good meal, a steak
dinner at Le Boeuf and some good booze, Jack
Daniels, and then went out to the Fillmore and
picked up a good-looking, young, Negro whore,
and he got laid in the Albert Bacon Fall Hotel.

The next day he went down to a fancy
stationery store on Market Street and bought
himself a thirty-dollar fountain pen, one with a
gold nib.

He showed it to me and said, 'Write with this,
but don't write hard because this pen has got

a gold nib, and a gold nib is very
impressionable. After a while it takes on the
personality of the writer. Nobody else can
write with it. This pen becomes just like a
person's shadow. It's the only pen to have.
But be careful.'

I thought to myself what a lovely nib trout
fishing in America would make with a stroke of
cool green trees along the river's shore, wild
flowers and dark fins pressed against the paper.

PRELUDE TO THE MAYONNAISE CHAPTER

'The Eskimos live among ice all their lives but
have no single word for ice.' - Man: His First
Million Years, by M.F. Ashley Montagu
    'Human language is in some ways similar to,
but in other ways vastly different from, other
kinds of animal communication. We simply have no
idea about its evolutionary history, though
many people have speculated about its possible
origins. There is, for instance, the "bow-bow"
theory, that language started from attempts to
imitate animal sounds. Or the "ding-dong"
theory, that it arose from natural
sound-producing responses. Or the "pooh-pooh"
theory, that it began with violent outcries and
exclamations ... We have no way of knowing
whether the kinds of men represented by the
earliest fossils could talk or not ... Language
does not leave fossils, at least not until it
has become written ...' - Man in Nature, by
Marston Bates
    'But no animal up a tree can initiate a

culture.' - 'The Simian Basis of Human
Mechanics,' in <u>Twilight of Man</u>, by Earnest
Albert Hooton

Expressing a human need, I always wanted to
write a book that ended with the word
Mayonnaise.

THE MAYONNAISE CHAPTER

                    Feb 3-1952
Dearest Florence and Harv.

    I just heard from Edith about
the passing of Mr Good. Our heart
goes out to you in deepest sympathy
Gods will be done. He has lived a
good long life and he has gone to
a better place. You were expecting
it and it was nice you could see
him yesterday even if he did not
know you. You have our prayers
and love and we will see you soon.
    God bless you both.

                    Love Mother and Nancy.

P.S.
Sorry I forgot to give you the mayonaise.